Of Mice and Nutcrackers

A Peeler Christmas

Richard Scrimger

illustrated by
Linda Hendry

D0103458

Tundra Books

Text copyright © 2001 by Richard Scrimger
Illustrations copyright © 2001 by Linda Hendry

Published in Canada by Tundra Books,
481 University Avenue, Toronto, Ontario M5G 2E9

Published in the United States by Tundra Books of Northern New York,
P.O. Box 1030, Plattsburgh, New York 12901

Library of Congress Card Number: 2001086860

All rights reserved. The use of any part of this publication reproduced,
transmitted in any form or by any means, electronic, mechanical,
photocopying, recording, or otherwise, or stored in a retrieval system,
without the prior written consent of the publisher – or, in case of
photocopying or other reprographic copying, a licence from the
Canadian Copyright Licensing Agency – is an infringement
of the copyright law.

National Library of Canada Cataloguing in Publication Data

Scrimger, Richard, 1957-
    Of mice and nutcrackers : a Peeler Christmas

ISBN 0-88776-498-3

I. Hendry, Linda.   II. Title.

PS8587.C74503 2001   jC813'.54   C2001-930267-3
PZ7.S370f 2001

We acknowledge the support of the Canada Council for the Arts and the
Ontario Arts Council for our publishing program.

We acknowledge the financial support of the Government of Canada
through the Book Publishing Industry Development Program for our
publishing activities.

Design by Ingrid Paulson
Printed and bound in Canada

1 2 3 4 5 6   06 05 04 03 02 01

To Jim Ellieff

ACKNOWLEDGMENTS

The idea for a sequel to *The Way to Schenectady* was Linda Granfield's. I thanked her. She convinced my publisher, Kathy Lowinger, who thought it should be a seasonal story. I agreed. My agent, Dean Cooke, suggested that I hurry up and write it this year. I said okay. My wife, Bridget, who reads all my stuff first, worried about the balance of the big scene. I saw her point. My daughter Thea insisted that one of the names be changed. I changed it. My editor, Sue Tate, wanted an entire day to discuss inconsistencies. I gave it to her.

And you thought a writer's life was lonely and pure.

Seriously, I'd like to thank all of the above for their contributions. Also, everyone connected with the Northumberland Players' 2001 production of *A Funny Thing Happened on the Way to the Forum* for letting me onstage, showing me a great time, and even trying to teach me — would you believe it? — to dance.

1

Waiting Room

The baby next to me sounds like a machine gun. *Ack ack ack ack ack.* She's an ugly baby: almost bald, with gummy brown eyes, a bubbling nose, and a wide-open toothless mouth. Her tonsils waggle as she coughs again. *Ack ack ack ack ack.*

"There, there, sweet pea," says her mom.

Sweet pea.

The hospital walk-in clinic is filled with coughers. Also sniffers and wheezers, moaners and drippers. It's December. Flu season. Kids clutch dirty toys. Parents wipe runny noses. Cartoon characters stare down from the walls. They don't care. They've seen it all before.

"Peeler!" calls the nurse. She has orange hair and black eyebrows. Good makeup for Halloween. Too bad it was weeks ago. She should put on her Christmas makeup soon. "Bernard Peeler."

"Right here," says Dad. He's holding my kid brother Bernie in his arms. Bernie's one of the wheezers. That's why we're here.

I

His breathing was bad this morning, when I left for school, and it got worse through the day. Dad didn't even let Bill and me take off our coats when we got home from school. "We're taking Bernie to the hospital," he said, in that tone of voice that means *no arguing*.

I didn't say, "But I'm thirteen; I can stay home by myself." I didn't say, "But I have homework." I didn't say anything. I turned around and walked back out the front door.

Bill said, "Aye, aye, sir." He's been saying that for a while now. He thinks he's a sailor. Last summer he was an astronaut, always saying "roger," or "affirmative," or "Houston, we have a problem," but he's been watching a lot of sea stories on TV lately. And there's this comic book series set on a sailing ship, with cannons and cutlasses and mizzenmasts. Last month he changed his personal e-mail address from *Astrocoolboy* to *Not_unjolly_Roger*. I'm getting tired of larboard and starboard and splicing the main brace.

"Bernard Peeler!" says the nurse again.

Dad stands up. Bernie wheezes in his arms.

The ugly baby beside me goes off again. *Ack ack ack ack ack.*

Bill paces up and down in the waiting room. His pants are wet at the bottom from the crust of slush that covers the sidewalks. We were supposed to get a major snowfall last week, but it wasn't major, and it wasn't really snow. Now it isn't really anything at all.

He stops pacing suddenly – the way he does every-thing. He slumps into Dad's chair and picks up the nearest book. A fat one, with a lamp on the cover. Bill is eleven: not much of a reader, not like me, but he likes to pretend. He starts turning pages. I open my knapsack. I take out my "Nutcracker" notebook.

Usually *The Nutcracker* is a ballet, with music you recognize from "Bugs Bunny" or "Walt Disney." My mom took me to see it when I was seven. I don't remember anything about it except the strawberry ice cream at intermission. It came in a silver dish, and there was a rolled-up wafer cookie in the middle. *Mmmm!* Anyway, our class – 7E – is doing a musical play based on *The Nutcracker* at the winter concert next week. I'm the director because it was all my idea. I wrote it – actually, I wrote the words. Tchaikovsky wrote the music. My best friend Patti is Maria, the heroine. Miss Gonsalves, our teacher, plays the piano. We've been rehearsing in the classroom for weeks. Tomorrow we get our first chance onstage in the gym. I can hardly wait.

I go over my notes from today: *Justin likes doll too much.* Justin is a slender well-dressed boy who sits in the front row of the class and raises his eyebrows a lot. He plays Maria's brother Fritz, who gets an ugly nutcracker for Christmas. He's supposed to toss it aside because he'd rather play with his toy soldiers.

3

Only Justin can't help smoothing down the fur on our nutcracker doll's hat.

I wonder if we could get a different nutcracker doll. An uglier one. I'll ask Patti's mom. She works in a gift shop. And I'll tell Justin again.

Next note: a single name, circled twice. *Jiri*. Oh, dear. He only has five lines, but he keeps forgetting them. I probably shouldn't have given him a speaking part. I thought and thought about it. Patti was against the idea, but I like Jiri, and he begged me to give him something to say. I'll have to talk to him too.

Next note: a phone number. I'm supposed to remind Trinley's mom, who's sewing the costume for the Mouse King, that we need it next Monday. Also to remind her that Essa, who plays the part, is really small.

Directing is more complicated than you think. It's not just bossing people around.

Bill's lips are moving as he reads. His eyebrows are down, and his mouth is open. He really seems interested.

"What's the book about?" I say.

"A storm at sea."

Figures.

The nurse calls the machine-gun baby, who gives me one last cough on her way out. "There, there, sweet pea," says her mom.

I think about the atmosphere in the hospital waiting room: a thick soup of germs, spiced with menthol and eucalyptus and dirty diapers. I try to breathe very lightly, through my nose. Maybe, if I take little breaths, the germs won't find their way down into my lungs.

Brad from my class comes into the waiting room, with his mom. He has golden hair – not blond or yellow, but gold, like a sunset. I can't decide if I like Brad or not. He smiles a special smile at me, like he's more interested in what I have to say than anything else in the world. A personal-for-me smile – and that's nice. And then I'll see him talking to Miss Gonsalves, or to my friend Patti, and he'll have the same special smile on his face.

Patti doesn't like him. She says his hair is the same color as margarine.

Brad was fine in school this afternoon, but now he's holding one hand in the other, cradling it.

His mom is checking in with the nurse. "My name is Ogilvy!" she says, in a loud voice. "With an *O*."

How else could you spell the name? I wonder. Pogilvy – only the *P* is silent, like pneumonia. Or psoriasis. Or Psmith. I wonder if that's what the machine-gun baby has: pneumonia.

Hey, Brad notices me. I wave at him. He tries to wave back with his good hand, winces in pain. Poor guy.

"Who's that, dear?" asks his mom. She frowns in my direction.

"A friend of mine from school," says Brad.

His mom looks from me to Brad, then comes right up to where I'm standing. "What's your name?" she says.

I tell her.

She nods, filing me away. "I like to know all about Brad's friends," she says.

Not much to say to that.

"What happened to you?" I ask Brad.

He looks embarrassed. "Hangnail," he mutters at last.

"What?"

"A bad one. See?" He shows me. There's some blood on his middle finger.

"Oh, yes," I say.

Brad's mom stares at me.

"Looks like you should be okay for tomorrow's rehearsal, though." Of course Brad is the star – the handsome prince transformed into a nutcracker doll.

"Rehearsal?" Brad's mom makes it sound like a dirty word. The way I'd say "cockroach."

"Uh, Jane and I are doing a project together in school," says Brad. He shakes his head at me. Why? I wonder.

"What kind of project?" his mom asks. "Why do you need to *rehearse*?" Again she emphasizes the word.

"It's *The Nut –*" I begin, but Brad interrupts.

"About nuts," he says, quickly and loudly. "A project about nuts. For science class." He smiles at me – the special one.

"Nuts?" says his mom.

"Sure," I say quickly. I find myself playing along. I don't know why – maybe it's the smile. "Nuts. All about nuts. Peanuts, chestnuts, cashews. Say, Brad, I found out where Brazil nuts come from today. Do you know where Brazil nuts come from? I'll give you a hint."

"Ogilvy," says the nurse.

"Come on," says Brad, dragging his mom away. He looks back for a second, shrugs his shoulders. I wave good-bye.

Weird.

Bernie's looking better when he gets back. "Hi, Bill," he says. "Hi, Jane. I can breathe now. See?" He breathes in, and starts to cough.

"Careful," says Dad.

Dad's not looking so good. His face is redder than usual, and he's taking a long time doing up Bernie's snowsuit. His hand trembles on the zipper.

"Come on," I say to Bill.

"In a minute," he says. "This is interesting. The storm is so bad they're going to throw this guy John overboard."

"Why?"

"He's a stowaway, and they figure he brought the storm."

"What are you reading?" asks Dad, looking over.

Bill holds up the book with the lamp on the cover. The Bible.

Dad laughs. "That's not John, it's Jonah. With an *a*."

Bill peers at the page. "Oh, yeah," he says. "How did you know?"

"I used to go to Sunday school," says Dad. "Now, let's get home. It's almost dinnertime, and we have to get Bernie's prescription."

"Could I take this book with me?" asks Bill. "I want to finish the story."

"I think we have a copy at home," says Dad. "Somewhere."

A dark December evening with the streetlights on and a cold wind whistling up your sleeves and down your collar. I shiver. A shadow flits over the snow as we walk across the hospital parking lot. Big and black and spooky – the shadow, that is. The snow is white, though it looks blue in the streetlights. There isn't a lot of snow – just enough to cover the ground, and collect in the folds of the garbage bags piled high by the curb.

"Avast!" says Bill, grabbing my arm to stop me. He points up into a big bare tree behind us. "D'you see that bird?"

"No," I say.

Dad is pushing Bernie in the stroller. They're ahead of us. Dad's head is down. He's hunched over. From the back he looks like an old man.

"It's a raven," says Bill. "The bird of doom."

"Bill – shut up!" I say.

"They say the raven hovers around houses of ill luck. Someone inside . . . *that* place there is very ill." He points dramatically.

"Bill, that's the hospital," I say.

"You see!" he says. "That proves it."

I stare up into the tree. The bare branches look cold and spooky. "It's not a raven, anyway. It's a duck, or something."

"A raven," he insists.

I make a quacking sound. "The duck of doom!"

Bill snorts with laughter.

We stop at the big drugstore on Copernicus Street and get Bernie's prescription, and some cough drops for Dad – the kind that taste horrible. Bernie doesn't try to climb out of the stroller, like he usually does.

The houses are close together on our street. I can tell ours even from a distance because it and the house beside it – we share a roof – lean into each other, like friends with their arms linked. There's a light on in our house. The front door opens. A beam of gold shines out from the hall onto our front walk. Mom stands in the doorway. She must have been watching for us. The beam of golden light makes her red-brown hair shine like a halo. She waves. We wave back.

9

From right overhead comes the most hollow mournful croaking sound. Scary as anything. It sounds like an old coffin door swinging shut – right on you. I jump. So does Bill.

"That wasn't a duck," says Bill.

2

Dweedle-Dweedle-Dee

I dream that I'm bowling. I don't know why – I don't bowl very often, or very well. Mostly at someone else's birthday party. In my dream, just like real life, I keep bowling gutter balls. So does the person in the next lane over. And the lane beside that. The whole bowling alley is full of lousy bowlers – every ball ends up in the gutter. I hear Brad's voice. Maybe he's the guy in the next lane. *Maria*, he says. Is he talking to me? My name is not Maria.

Something scary about being Maria. I'm scared to turn my head and look at Brad. I run up to bowl again, grabbing firmly onto the ball, aiming right down the middle of the lane. I plant my feet and try to let go of the ball, only I can't. I hang on too long, and find myself at the other end of the alley, down by the pins. I'm small, and I'm in the gutter, and this giant bowling ball is coming right at me. I try to climb out of the gutter, but I can't. Of course it's a gutter ball, and it's coming, coming, coming. . . .

I wake up, sweating, and still afraid to turn my head. My heart is racing. Darkness. A flashing red light across the room – 3:05. My clock. I realize where I am. A sigh of relief – it was just a bad dream. I wonder if it was about *The Nutcracker*. Maria is the girl in the play.

I shake my head. I must be more worried about this production than I thought. That reminds me – I must remember to ask Brad what all that was about yesterday with his mom.

I get out of bed and go to the bathroom for a drink of water. No glass, so I bend down and gulp from the tap. And I hear a sound from next door, from the other side of the connecting wall. It's coming toward me, getting closer and closer. I choke on the water. I'm back in my dream. The sound is a bit like a bowling ball.

I listen hard. Marbles, I guess, is what it really is. Little Cisco, the kid next door, is rolling marbles up and down the hallway.

Marbles at three in the morning?

I stick my head into my brothers' rooms. Bernie's in a junior bed against the wall. He's sleeping on his back, still and calm. His hands are crossed on his chest, and his skin is blue-white, like skim milk. Bill is tossing and turning – dreaming of a storm at sea, perhaps.

I can hear my mom snoring from down the hall. A comforting night sound.

Marbles at three in the morning. Okay, I guess. It's not too noisy. Last year they dug up the street all night long for a month. That was noisy. I go back to bed.

Next morning Bernie is feeling a lot better. He comes bouncing into my bedroom, the way he usually does. "Hi, Jane," he says. "It snowed last night. It's all white outside."

I run to the window. Yup. Snow. The sun's just up, and the world looks clean and cold. People are scraping snow off the sidewalks and piling it on the lawns. You aren't allowed to pile the snow on the road because that's where the cars park. The people have mufflers around their heads. Their breath steams behind them, so they look like tug-boats in a busy harbor.

Bernie's running around in his pajamas.

"You should put socks on," I say to him.

"I'm fine. Except for a stuffy nose." He sniffs.

"You're still sick," I say. "You should get dressed."

"No."

He doesn't go to school yet, so he doesn't have to get dressed.

"Put on something warmer. A sweater, or a bathrobe, or something."

"Bossy," he says, running out of the room and downstairs. Oh, well.

I get dressed and head downstairs too.

Dad's smile is a bit smaller than usual. So is Dad, come to think of it. He's hunched over, and he clutches a big sweater around himself.

"Hi, honey, have some soft tack," he says.

"Bill's the one who likes soft tack." It's navy food – I don't know why they can't call it bread, but they don't. I get myself some cold cereal and milk. Bernie isn't allowed to have milk because of his stuffy nose. Dad pours him some juice and sits him in his booster seat at the table beside me.

"Can I put juice on my flakes, Daddy?" he asks.

I make a face. "Don't do it," I say.

"Dad, can I?"

"Sure," says Dad. "But remember, you have to eat it."

Bernie thinks for a moment, then acts carefully and deliberately. He takes a spoonful of dry cereal from his bowl, and holds it in midair. Then he pours a little bit of apple juice from his cup onto the spoonful of cereal.

Guess what happens.

"Oops," says Bernie.

I move out of the way. Our kitchen table is on a slant. Dad says it's not the table; the whole kitchen is on a slant. If you were eating spaghetti and meatballs, say, and a meatball fell off your plate and onto the kitchen table, it would roll off the table and onto the floor; and then, if you didn't pick it up,

14

your poor meatball would, as the song says, roll right out the door.

Apple juice is flowing toward me like a river. It's usually better to sit uphill from Bernie.

Bill wanders in. I can hear his bare feet slapping against the kitchen linoleum. "Where are my striped socks?" he asks Dad.

"I think I saw them last night in the bathroom," he says.

"You didn't wash them, did you?"

Dad shakes his head. He's mopping up Bernie's spill. Bill heads back out the door.

"Your tack is getting cold," Bernie calls after him. "It won't be soft anymore."

"Hard tack is good too." Bill heads upstairs.

Dad coughs. A bad cough. He sounds like the ugly baby in the doctor's office. *Ack ack ack ack ack.*

"There, there, sweet pea," I say.

"Yeah, yeah," says Dad.

A snowy day means that the school hallways are wet and slippery. I almost fall, getting into my school shoes. I have to grab onto Patti to steady myself. Her locker is beside mine.

"Careful!" she says.

Patti is a bit of a worrier. Perfect for the part of Maria in the play, the girl who cares for the poor nutcracker doll that her brother Fritz has broken so carelessly.

I'm hopping on one foot. My other one is wet. I hate wet feet. The bell rings.

"If you aren't careful, you'll knock us both over!" Patti spits when she talks because of her braces. They're new, and she's not used to them yet. Her dark eyebrows curve down. "Come on, clumsy, we're going to be late!"

"Now, now, you girls!" Mr. March has a smile on his face and a mop in his hands. He works harder than anyone else in the school, I think. He makes the hallway clean around us while I struggle into my shoes.

"Sorry, Mr. March," I say. Funny, it didn't occur to me to say sorry to Patti. Maybe because I'm not marking up her nice clean floor. Maybe because she isn't smiling.

There's a series of black boot marks going down the middle of the hall. Mr. March wipes them with his mop, but they don't come away.

Language arts is right after lunch recess. Today we're trying to run through the whole play, so we can be ready for our rehearsal in the gym this afternoon. We're in the middle of the second scene when I notice something important.

"Stop!" I call. "Patti, I think you've fallen off the stage!"

Our classroom is in the old part of the school. The wooden desks are planted in rows, like the crosses in

Flanders fields, and cannot be moved. No matter how we lay it out, there are always a few desks in the middle of the stage area. In trying to step around a desk, Patti has fallen into the audience.

"Sorry," she says.

"Remember to keep upstage, so that you don't have to turn away from the audience to look at Michael." Michael is Herr Stahlbaum, Fritz and Maria's godfather. He's the one who brings the nutcracker. Michael's a strange guy – he laughs a lot, but he's angry too. His voice is deep and raspy. A big, funny bully is what he is.

Do I mean that? Bully? I think so. He laughs when people fall down, and he punches a lot. That's a bully, I guess.

"Upstage? You mean back," says Patti. "You want me to keep back."

"Yes," I say.

Michael snorts and rolls his eyes – sorry, his one eye. The other one has a patch on it.

Miss Gonsalves turns to me. We're the only ones on chairs. The rest of the class is either onstage, or waiting to go on.

"What do you think, Jane? Should they do it one more time?"

I frown at my notebook. "There's a lot to go through," I say. "I'll make a note about Patti staying upstage, and Michael speaking a bit more slowly."

"Hey!" says Michael.

"Good idea, Jane." Miss Gonsalves smiles at Michael. She's almost the only one who can. She and Jiri.

"It's this stupid classroom," says Patti. "I'll do better when we get on a real stage."

"Of course you will," says Miss Gonsalves warmly.

I can't decide what I want to be when I grow up, but Miss Gonsalves is one option. She's smart and she wears neat clothes and is never *never* upset. And she's gorgeous. If I end up like Miss Gonsalves, I'll be pretty happy.

She likes me too. She likes everyone. That's what's so great about her. She even smiles when Michael pushes his way into class, slams his books on the desk, and frowns like a thundercloud.

Essa used to sit in front of Michael. She said she could feel how angry he was, all the time. "It was like a furnace," she said. Of course Miss Gonsalves likes Essa, who is the smallest grade 7 you ever saw. Smaller than you, if you're reading this by yourself. Smaller than most grade 4s. Michael could pick her up and carry her under one arm like a bread stick. Not that Miss Gonsalves would let him.

Zillah sits in front of Michael now. Zillah, all in black, who never says a word. She doesn't seem to notice the anger.

★

"Places!" I call. "Patti and Michael, we'll start where the clock strikes midnight." I check the stage. The nutcracker doll is on one of the "onstage" desks, and the grandfather clock – actually an old chest of drawers, with a big cardboard clock face taped on top – is at the back, near the blackboard. "Now, Patti, it's Christmas Eve and everyone's asleep. You've been woken up. You go downstairs in the middle of the night, and suddenly you see your godfather sitting on top of your old clock. How do you feel?"

"Surprised?" lisps Patti.

Michael laughs again. "You think?" he says. "This old geezer comes out of my clock, I'd be surprised too."

The class laughs. I feel stupid. "Let's see if we can get all the way through the magic spell," I say. "Let's go. Patti, downstage center. Brad, get ready. You're on in a minute. For now you're under the table. Michael, you're –"

"On top of the clock," he says, in a loud voice.

Another laugh.

"Right. That's, um, upstage center. Okay, Patti, take it from your line 'Oh, oh, oh.' And – action."

The music changes now: deeper, slower. You know this bit. It's really famous. *Dweedle-dweedle*-dee, *dee-doo*-dee, *dah doo dee*, dah-*dah-dah*, doo-*doo-doo*, doh-*doh-doh*, dah-*dee*-dah-*dee*-doh.

Well, that's the way I hear it. I don't read music.

Jiri looks excited. He recognizes the tune. He elbows his way forward. Oh, no. I hold up my hand to stop him, but he's onstage now, facing Patti like I told him to, smiling, and following his musical cue with enthusiasm.

"Welcome, Princess, to the North.
I . . . uh . . . welcome you to . . . ding it!"

Jiri always says "ding it!" when he's upset.

Michael sighs. Patti frowns. The music stops.

"Wait!" I call. "We'll try that again. Jiri! Remember what we talked about last time?"

He hangs his head now. He remembers. "Not my cue yet?"

"Not yet," I say. "You're at the very end of the play. That dance music comes back a few times. Remember?"

"It is the correct music?"

"Oh, yes. You got the music part right."

He beams.

"But it's the wrong time. You must wait. Stand next to me, and I'll tell you when to go on. Okay?"

"Sorry, Jane. Ding it!" he says.

Ding it! is right.

Miss Gonsalves catches my eye. In her face is a hint of worry – the first I've ever seen.

"Nice try, Jiri!" she says brightly.

3

A Voice from the Wall

1:45. Second-last period of the day. Geography. Miss Gonsalves sits on her desk, legs crossed neatly.

"What's latitude?" She spins her globe around and around. A couple of hands go up. Not mine. I stare at the clock. Thirty minutes until our *Nutcracker* rehearsal.

"How would you define latitude, Patti?"

"Is it . . . width?" Patti sprays gently.

"Width?"

"Well, the lines on the globe go sideways."

"So that longitude would be height? Is that it?" Miss Gonsalves laughs. A beautiful gurgling laugh, very infectious. Justin, in paisley today, giggles. Essa, beside Justin, smiles up at him. "An ingenious idea, Patti."

I check the clock again. Twenty-eight minutes.

Michael laughs meanly. Miss Gonsalves keeps smiling, and walks down the row to his desk. "And what do you think, Michael?"

He glowers up at her. Her smile doesn't change a bit. "Latitude," she prompts him. "Right now you are sitting on forty-four degrees north latitude. What does that make latitude?"

"If he's *sitting* on it," begins Jiri. "Then it might be . . ."

"Might be what, Jiri?"

Jiri doesn't know, of course. He's the biggest kid in the class, even bigger than Michael; and the nicest kid, but he's not smart at all. If Essa is a puny body and a giant brain, Jiri is the other way around. He should probably be back in grade 2 or 3, but he's always been with this class, and we'd miss him. He spends a lot of time with a resource teacher.

"Yes, Jiri?"

He frowns, concentrating. His hair tumbles off his head in cascades, like a waterfall. He pushes it back with a big sweaty hand. His veins stand out, like a man's. A strong man's.

"It's not . . . a chair, is it?"

"Latitude? No, not quite."

"Ding it!" He looks down.

You'd expect Michael to make fun of Jiri, but he doesn't. No one does – not even the real bullies. Last year a huge kid from high school kicked a neighborhood cat that Jiri was playing with. Jiri broke the kid's arm.

Five minutes before the last period, Miss Gonsalves asks us to tidy off our desks. She reminds us to bring in an authentic artifact from the 1950s for our history diorama. I don't know what to bring. I wonder if my dad would count as an artifact. He was born in the 1950s.

"And now, class, I want you to take out your *Nutcracker* scripts. We'll be going to the gymnasium for last period."

The gym is where the stage is. This will be our first rehearsal onstage. Miss Gonsalves told me how much trouble she had arranging it. Mr. Gebohm hates to have the gym used for anything except sports.

Michael cheers. Miss Gonsalves tells him to shush. "Let's work hard today. We only have forty minutes because there's a basketball practice right after school."

The clock ticks. One minute to the bell. Miss Gonsalves nods to me. I'm in charge now. I stand up, clear my throat. And get interrupted before I can open my mouth.

Miss Gonsalves.

A stern voice coming from the wall.

Miss Gonsalves, are you there?

It's the intercom. Miss Gonsalves raises her voice. "Yes, Mrs. Winter?"

Are Jane Peeler and Brad Ogilvy in your class right now?

I look up.

"Yes, Mrs. Winter."

Send them to the office, please. Right away.

Of course Michael snickers. "Jane and Brad, ha-ha-ha." He's the loudest, but he's not the only one.

23

I start blushing. Why? Is Brad blushing? I don't know. I'm not looking at him.

Patti smiles at me uncertainly. Then at Brad. Then she looks back at me, but she's not smiling anymore.

"I'll do that, Mrs. Winter," says Miss Gonsalves out loud. Then, quieter, to us, "Better get going, you two. See you in the gym when you're finished."

And of course that starts Michael off again. "You two. Ha-ha-ha."

The hallways are clean, except for a fresh line of dirty scuff marks down the middle. From the classrooms come smells of chalk and wet wool, sounds of incomprehension and exasperation.

Brad walks quickly. I trot to keep up. Not that I have to, no reason to think we're together. But I do. *You two.* I'd like to talk to Brad, but I don't really know how to open the conversation.

"How's the hangnail?" I ask finally.

"Better." He doesn't turn around. The back of his neck is red. He might be blushing.

I wonder what the principal wants us for. Last year I was called to the office because they couldn't read Dad's handwriting on a form. But Brad and me – why single us out?

Turns out we're not the only ones who were called to the office. My brother Bill's there, too.

All right, I give up. What could it be?

Bill gives me a look. A little-brother-to-big-sister look. The one that says *now what have you got me into?* I shrug my shoulders.

Our principal's name is Mr. Gordon. He's young, for a principal. He dresses young, in jeans and sweatshirts, and he actually likes you to call him by his first name, which is Gordon too. Gordon Gordon. I can't imagine what his parents were thinking.

He's a bald guy, with eyebrows that jump up and down when he talks. He makes jokes – and he doesn't seem to mind when no one laughs. I'd say that he isn't bad, for a principal, which I suppose is like saying that corn isn't bad, for a vegetable; or that the measles booster isn't bad, for a needle.

Right now he's looking concerned. His eyebrows are pointing down. He tells us good afternoon, and then asks how we're feeling. It's a formal question – *how are you all feeling?* His eyebrows crawl along the ridge of bone over his eye sockets, like fuzzy caterpillars looking for each other. I picture them meeting in the middle of his face.

"I feel fine," says Brad.

"Me, too," I say.

The principal nods at Bill. "And you? You feel fine too?"

"Aye, aye, sir," says Bill.

Gordon stares down at a piece of paper in his hand. "This is a public health notice from Our Lady

Of Mercy Hospital," he says. "They want to see everyone who was in the pediatrics walk-in clinic last night. Your names were all on their computer."

My mouth drops open. So that's it. That's what we've got in common. The waiting room with the germs and the ugly baby.

"That true?" Gordon asks. "You three were there last night? Brad Ogilvy, Bill Peeler, Jane Peeler?"

We nod. Is it my imagination, or does the principal roll his big office chair farther away from his desk? Farther away from us?

"I'm sure it's just a precaution," he says, "but we're going to send you home early. And you're to stay at home until the hospital tests come back."

I'm not worried about the hospital. I feel fine. I say the first thing on my mind. "You can't send us home," I say. "Not Brad and me. What about our rehearsal?"

"Rehearsal?"

"For the winter concert. Our class is doing *The Nutcracker*."

"Oh, yes. Mr. Gebohm was in here complaining about that."

"I'm directing, and Brad here is the star."

"Well, you'll just have to miss it."

"But we can't. How can we practice *The Nutcracker* without the Nutcracker?"

Brad, I notice, isn't saying anything. In fact, he's looking relieved. Like he wants to miss rehearsal.

26

"Don't worry," says the principal. "Miss Gonsalves is a very talented person. She'll manage without you."

"But it's our first chance onstage!"

There's a knock at the door, and Mrs. Winter pops her head in. She's the office secretary – very efficient, very busy, not exactly cheerful. You know her. You've probably got her at your school too.

"They're here," she says, with a meaningful nod. She's holding a handkerchief.

Gordon stands up. "Your parents have come to pick you up," he says to us. "Your father, Jane and Bill, and your mother, Brad."

As we file past Mrs. Winter, she raises her handkerchief to block her face.

What is going on? What are we supposed to have?

4

"It's a sign"

It's not far to the hospital. We walk down Copernicus Street. When we pass the fruit store that sells Christmas trees, Bernie asks when we'll get our tree, and Dad doesn't answer. When we get to the big automatic door, Bernie climbs out of his stroller and runs ahead. He knows where to go. What with ear infections, stomach upsets, and sore throats, we've spent plenty of time at the hospital.

Today's different. The glass doors with the picture of Goofy are locked. There's a guard outside. "You folks looking for the kids' clinic?" he asks.

"We were here yesterday," says Dad. "We –"

"Down the hall," says the guard. "Radiology."

I notice a sign on the wall outside the clinic: CONTAMINATED AREA.

"I thought Bernie was getting better," I whisper to Dad.

"Me, too," he says. His face is pinched and gray.

Brad and his mom are ahead of us in line. I wave. He nods back. His mom turns to stare. She has her arm around him, as if she's afraid he'll escape. "Oh, it's you," she says. "The nut girl."

Radiology is X-rays. Pretty cool. I get to wear a heavy lead apron and stand in front of what looks like a laser gun. *Zzzap.* Then it's Bill's turn. Then Dad's and Bernie's. Bernie has to stand on a chair. *Zzzap*!

That's it.

I don't feel sick. I don't look sick. I don't see anyone who looks sick.

I check around for sweet pea, the ugly baby; can't find her.

And then we go home. Tough work walking through the unshoveled stretches of sidewalk. Poor Dad – even tougher pushing the stroller through the snow. Bernie climbs in and out, trying to help. Bill slouches along. I'm preoccupied.

What if the X-rays show that I'm sick? What if I have to stay at home? I'll miss rehearsals. I'll have to miss the show. That can't happen.

What if Brad is sick? No one else would be as good.

I wonder how rehearsal went without me and Brad? I hope Michael didn't overdo his part. At the last rehearsal, he put on a "godfather" accent – as if he were making Fritz and Maria an offer they couldn't refuse. Miss Gonsalves laughed and laughed, and Michael actually blushed.

We'll have to arrange a rehearsal schedule. The show is a week away. Five school days. At least two or three rehearsals will have to be onstage.

"There it is, Dad – see it?" Bill's eyes are wide. He points.

In our front yard is a big old maple tree. It's a great tree. I love the shade it provides in the summer. The leaves that fall off it in the autumn cover our small front lawn waist-deep. It's a home for squirrels and bats and cicadas. It's bare now, of course. I can see the house beside ours through the bare black branches.

On a low branch is a huge black bump – a lump bigger than any squirrel I've ever encountered. It's practically the size of a small bear.

"Do you see, Dad?" says Bill.

"I see it," says Bernie, looking in the wrong direction.

Dad frowns. "What is it?"

As I watch, the bump unfolds a gigantic pair of wings, and flaps slowly toward us. It's a crow. A huge crow. Or maybe, a raven. Bernie shrieks, and hides against Dad. The crow looks big enough to carry him off.

"It's a sign," whispers Bill.

I've had enough of this.

"No, Bill," I say. "*That's* a sign." I point to the STOP sign on the corner. "And *those* are signs." I point to a telephone pole with NO PARKING and speed limit

signs. Bill doesn't say anything. "What you're pointing at, Bill, is a bird. Not a sign. Okay? Enough with
this silly superstition."

I don't know why I'm so upset. Maybe it's because
superstitions are so negative. Walk under a ladder,
break a mirror, spill the salt, cross a black cat – you
could wreck your whole future in a morning. Why
must evil always win?

"It's in our front yard," says Bill. "A bad luck sign.
Someone is ill. Very ill."

"But Bernie's better," I say. "And what about all the good luck signs? Ever hear the one about the front porch? A sagging front porch is good luck – did you know that? So is a cracked front walk. So is a burnt-out lightbulb."

"Is that really true?" asks Bernie, his eyes wide. He checks out the porch, the front walk. Our porch light has been burnt out for ages. Dad keeps saying he'll have to change it one of these days.

"It's as really true as anything Bill says about ravens. Gee, I wonder if we have a pizza coupon in our mailbox – you have no idea how lucky that is!"

I reach up to check and guess what? We do.

"Wow! We must be the luckiest family in the world!" says Bernie.

Dad is having trouble lifting the stroller onto the sagging front porch. He starts to laugh, then breaks off to cough.

Bill's friend David is a familiar sight at our house. He doesn't bother to knock. He practically has his own coat hook in the front hall. Today, though, Dad won't let him use it.

"Go back home," he says, taking the new parka off the hook and holding it out so that David can slide his arms back into it. "Maybe you can come over tomorrow. Better call first, to make sure."

"What's wrong, Mr. P?" he asks. He calls Dad Mr. P for Peeler. Bill calls David's mom Mrs. B – for Bergmann. Dad thinks it's funny.

"Bill may be sick, David. We all may be sick. We had to go to the hospital for tests this afternoon, to find out. You better stay away until the hospital calls us back."

Bill is halfway down the stairs. He waves. David waves back.

"He doesn't look sick, Mr. P."

"And I don't feel sick, Dad," says Bill. "Can't David stay? Please? We're on the eighth level of *Norbert's World. The Dog's Nose.*"

He's talking about a computer game – you're an alien from Jupiter and you have to find missing treasure. I don't play those kind of games. I prefer the ones where you solve problems, or rule the universe.

"Sorry, son. We're in quarantine here for a bit. Say hi to your parents for me, David. Maybe Bill will be in school tomorrow."

David clumps down the porch steps. Bill waves, then turns excitedly.

"Quarantine? Did you mean it, Dad? Are we in quarantine?"

"Afraid so. There was a severe case of pneumonia in the clinic last night. They want to make sure there aren't any more."

"Cool! We can hoist the checkered flag! That'll tell people to steer clear of us. We'll be like the plague ship!"

"Great," I say.

I am not sick. I am not sick. I am not sick.

Dad smiles wanly. "Are you sure you're not getting quarantine mixed up with car racing, son?" he says. "In car racing, the winner gets a checkered flag. There are no winners in infectious diseases."

Bill runs away upstairs.

Bernie wants to play a game. We decide on hide-and-seek. I start off counting in the kitchen. Dad can't play because he has to make dinner.

"Feel like rice?" he asks me.

"You mean all gluey and burnt and stuck to the bottom of the pot? No, I feel fine. I'm not sick. I don't feel like rice at all."

Dad smiles, dumps some rice and butter into a pot of water and puts it on the stove to boil. Then he opens the fridge door and starts rooting around.

"What are you looking for?" I ask.

"Leftovers to go with the rice."

"Seventeen, eighteen, nineteen," I say loudly.

The phone rings. Dad hurries to answer – which isn't like him. "Hello – oh, hang on a second." He gives the phone to me.

It's Patti. She tells me that Miss Gonsalves didn't bother to hold the rehearsal. They just read over their lines again, in class, and Jiri forgot his. "You're going to have to replace him," she says. "I don't like him."

I don't say anything. I'm thinking that we are going to have to find a way to get onstage really soon.

"Well, see you tomorrow at school," she lisps. "You and . . . Brad." She hangs up.

Dad is leaning over the counter. His eyes are closed.

"Twenty! Ready or not, Bernie, here I come!" I call.

I push open the swing door into the family room. I look behind the door and under the dresser with the TV on it and behind the long curtains and under the piano bench, with all the discarded sheet music and scraps of paper that have fallen off the piano. I even check – carefully, from a distance – the tall skinny bookcase. (Bernie recently discovered that he could climb the bookcase, using the shelves as a ladder. One afternoon he perched there, like an eagle, nearly scaring the life out of me when he leapt down on me.) I can't find Bernie.

Dad wanders in. He's sweating, but it isn't that hot. "I think I'll have a little rest," he says, making for the couch. "Keep an eye on things, would you, Jane? And call me when the rice is ready. I'll take it off the stove."

"How will I know the rice is ready?"

"It'll be all gluey and burnt and stuck to the bottom of the pot." He smiles. "That should be in about half an hour."

"Dad, are you all right?"

"Oh, sure."

Bill comes running downstairs carrying a big piece of poster board. He shows it to us: a series of black and yellow diamonds. "It's the plague flag," he explains. "Fly that in the front window and all the other ships'll steer clear."

Plague. Great.

"Very nice," says Dad. He settles himself slowly onto the couch. It's green and shiny, and it sags in the middle. He sighs, sort of scrunching himself against the pile of pillows at one end. His feet go up, his head falls back, and his eyes close – momentarily.

Then they fly open again.

"Help!" A muffled voice coming from nearby. I can't tell where, exactly. "Help, Daddy! Help, Jane!"

Bernie's voice.

"What the –" says Dad.

"Bernie!" I cry. "Where are you?"

I wonder if he's gone away somewhere to lie down. Maybe he has the plague.

Bill is staring around the room. "I saw a show once, where aliens hid a girl inside the TV," he says. "The family turned on the TV and there she was."

Bill and I cross the room to our TV. "Bernie! Bernie! Are you in there?" Bill turns the set on. A game show. We look carefully. Bernie is not one of the contestants.

"Hey! Help, Bill!"

Where is Bernie's voice coming from?

"The radio!" Bill dashes into the kitchen.

Dad is struggling up into a sitting position.

"Keep talking, Bernie!" I call.

"Are you in the radio?" Bill asks loudly.

"No," says Bernie's voice.

"Where are you?"

"I'm underneath Dad! Help!"

Dad is sitting up now. There's a commotion in the pile of pillows behind him, and a head covered in tousled brown hair pops out. Bernie was hiding in the sofa cushions. Dad must have almost squashed him.

"Sorry, little guy," he says.

With difficulty, Bernie climbs out. "Whew!" he says, and then sniffs. "What's for dinner?" he asks.

"Rice pilaf," says Dad.

"What's pilaf?"

I can answer that. "Leftovers," I say.

They turn out to be pretty good. The rice isn't over-cooked. Mom's home in time for dessert, which is brownies and ice cream. Like I said, pretty good.

Mom's a little worried when we tell her about visiting the hospital. She reaches across the table to feel Bernie's forehead and asks how he's feeling.

"Still a bit squished," he says.

"Squished?"

"Ah, that would be my fault," Dad explains. "I sat on him."

Mom spoons some ice cream carefully. She's still wearing her work clothes. She doesn't want to get them dirty.

5

Breakfast

I'm wide awake in the dark. My heart is pounding. I'm scared. Something woke me – something familiar, but I don't remember what. I want to go and see Mom and Dad. Then I remember I can't.

The hospital called before I went to bed. Good news: I don't have pneumonia. Neither do Bernie and Bill. Bad news: Dad does. He's really sick.

Because this pneumonia is infectious, he's supposed to stay in isolation. By himself. Mom has set up the third-floor office as his sick headquarters. Dad tried to help her, carrying some bedding up the narrow rickety stairs. He started coughing and coughing, so hard that he couldn't breathe. *Ack ack ack ack ack ack ack ack ack ack ack.* After that, Mom wouldn't let him help anymore.

So now when I wake up scared, I don't want to bother Dad, who's sick; and I don't want to bother Mom, who's tired out.

There's the sound again, unmistakable. I breathe a sigh of relief. It's only Cisco, playing in his room next door. Rolling his marbles up and down, up and down.

Marbles at midnight. I'm going to have to talk to him, or his mom. What kind of bedtime is midnight for a kindergartner? I go back to sleep.

I get up as if this were any winter morning, frost on the window, old snow on the ground. I brush my teeth like normal, and dress for school. The hospital said that Bill and I can go. We're healthy. Bill isn't pleased to be healthy, but I am. I've got to talk to Principal Gordon about rehearsals.

I do hope Brad isn't infected. What would we do for a hero? There aren't too many guys in our class. Michael is all wrong for the Nutcracker, and besides, we need him for the Godfather. Jiri would never remember all the Nutcracker lines. Justin – no. He's a nice guy, but a bit too . . . well, not exactly a nutcracker. A nutbender, maybe.

I run downstairs. And get a surprise. Mom is in the kitchen, in her bathrobe. Bernie's in his booster seat, fiddling with a bowl of oatmeal.

"Hi, Mom!" I run over and give her a hug. I almost never see her in the morning. She has an important job, telling city hall what they ought to do about housing. Advising, she calls it. Most days she's out of the house before I'm awake.

She kisses the top of my head.

"Where's Dad?" I ask.

"Still in bed." She spoons oatmeal into a bowl for me.

"Did you make this, Mom?" I ask. "I didn't know you could cook."

She gives me a funny kind of smile. "Of course I can cook," she says.

"Great," I say.

"I used to cook all the time. Who says I can't cook? Does your father say I can't cook?"

"No, no. It's just that . . . well, you don't cook. Not much."

"Well, I made this oatmeal. I also made your lunch."

"Thanks," I say. "What is for lunch today? I hope it's not tuna."

Tuna is what we get when Dad hasn't time to think of anything interesting. There's always a can of tuna in the cupboard. Bill doesn't like tuna either. Cat food sandwiches, he calls them.

Mom doesn't say anything.

Bernie coughs, and pushes his bowl away. "Mom," he begins.

Bill clatters downstairs calling out that he can't find any clean shirts. His skinny arms and chest are covered in goose bumps. He stops at the sight of Mom. And opens his mouth.

"Isn't there anything in your drawer?" she asks. Her voice reminds me of the frosted kitchen window: beautiful, but cold.

"Mom," says Bernie. "This cereal is bumpy."

The phone rings.

"Eat it," she says.

"Do I have to eat oatmeal?" asks Bill, shivering.

"Dad usually makes toast for Bill," I explain to Mom's back.

"Hard tack," he says. "Not toast."

The phone rings again. Mom picks it up.

I take a bite of oatmeal. Bernie's right. It tastes terrible. Full of bumps. I make a face and swallow.

"How's Dad?" Bill asks.

Mom frowns. "They can't do that," she says into the phone. "They don't have permission from the council. I circulated a memo."

"How's Dad?" Bill asks.

"Still in bed," I answer.

Mom looks over. "Hurry, Bill. Get dressed and eat your breakfast. School starts in half an hour." She goes back to the phone. "You tell them that from me," she says.

"But my long-sleeved shirts are all dirty," says Bill. "And I don't like ordinary oatmeal."

"And if you thought you didn't like ordinary oatmeal," I mutter, "wait until you try this."

Mom doesn't hear me. "I won't be in this morning," she says into the phone.

Bernie's been quiet for a while. Now he squinches himself around, and slides out of the bottom of his booster seat. He's been practicing that move for a while.

"I have to go now," he says.

He doesn't mean he has to leave. And he doesn't mean he has to go to school; he's not old enough. What he has to do is go to the bathroom. He's pretty good about remembering. This past summer we went on a trip to Auntie Vera's, and he kept forgetting. He's much better now. He doesn't wear a diaper, and he almost never makes mistakes.

"Good for you, Bernie," I tell him. He goes over to Mom. Tugs on her robe.

"Can I have toast too, Mom?" I say. "I'll make it." I take a loaf of bread from the bread drawer, and a bread knife from the cutlery drawer.

"Hang on!" says Mom. To the phone or us? I can't tell.

"Please, Mom," says Bernie. "Now."

Mom stands there in the middle of the kitchen. The phone quivers in one hand. The wooden spoon quivers in the other hand. Porridge drips onto the floor.

Bill is shivering. Bernie is tugging on her bathrobe. I am cutting a slice of bread from the loaf.

"STOP!" Mom cries. "Everybody, stop right now!"

We all stop moving. The ticking of the clock is very loud.

She bangs down the phone.

"Jane, put *down* that knife. Right away. Put away the bread and eat your porridge. Bill, put on yesterday's shirt. Right away. Then eat your breakfast and go to school. Bill and Jane, your lunches are on the table." She picks up Bernie.

"What's for lunch?" Bill asks.

Mom runs out of the kitchen without answering. I catch sight of Bernie's face over her shoulder. It's all scrunched up. I know what that means – she's *too late*.

I catch Bill's eye. "Tuna for lunch, I bet," I say.

He sighs. "Cat food sandwiches."

I look all around for Brad on the playground before school. Don't find him. I do see Cisco from next door, playing on the wooden climbing apparatus. He and a bunch of kindergarten friends are rolling along the upper level of the climber toward what used to be a slide. The school board took the slide down because it was dangerous, and put up a ladder instead. No one uses the ladder. Now there's a drop-off to nothing. Closer and closer the little kids roll. I wonder if they'll stop in time.

One of the girls doesn't. She rolls off the edge of the platform, and drops right in front of me, on her bottom. She laughs heartily. So do all the other kids. Kindergartners are pretty tough.

"Hey, Cisco," I call.

He's lying down covered in snow, from his tuque to his toes. "Hi," he says.

"Cisco, were you up late last night? Real late?"

I think he frowns. His scarf is in the way. "How did you know?" he asks, getting slowly to his feet. He's on the platform, so he's taller than me. My head is level with his knees.

"I heard you," I say. "You were rolling marbles up and down the hall. You've done it before, too. Why were you doing that?"

But he's shaking his head. "Wasn't," he says.

"Trucks, then. Or bowling bowls. You were rolling something."

"Nuh-uh."

The little girl who fell is climbing up the ladder to the platform. She slips on one of the rungs, and falls back onto the snow at my feet. She laughs, then climbs back to her feet and attacks the ladder again.

I help her up.

"Cisco, I live next door. I heard you."

He keeps shaking his head.

I see Brad across the school yard. He's not infected. Good.

He's talking to Patti. She's real close, and leaning closer. As I watch, she puts her hand on his arm.

"At Homey's," says Cisco. Or something like that – it's hard to hear past his scarf.

"What?"

He says the word clearer this time. "I stayed at Omi's. All night."

I stare. "So you weren't even home?"

"Nuh-uh," he says.

44

"What about your mom? Was she home?" Cisco doesn't have a dad. At least, I suppose he does, but I've never seen him.

"Nuh-uh."

"The house was empty? Your whole house?"

He squinches up his eyes. "Uh-huh," he says, and trudges away.

I think about the house next door to mine, separated from me by only a thin wall. I think about the sound I heard last night, and the night before. Could I have imagined it? Could it all be fake? I think back.

Nope. Or, in Cisco's words, nuh-uh.

So I am forced to think about a strange presence on the other side of that wall. Burglars? Ghosts? What? I don't know.

Whatever it is, that *thing* on the other side of the wall is playing marbles.

The bell rings.

6

Etceteras

Gordon Gordon sounds particularly jolly, reading our morning announcements. *Today is Wednesday. Fourteen days to Christmas. Five days to Chanukah. Fifteen days to Kwanzaa. Cody in grade 2 has a birthday. Milk money is due the day after tomorrow. The boys' basketball team has a practice at lunch. And –* he chortles *– there will be a surprise in the library today.* He chortles again and hangs up.

Of course we all want to know what the surprise is, but Miss Gonsalves just winks and says we'll find out soon enough.

"Is it a kitty?" asks Jiri.

"No."

"Well, would you like a kitty, Miss Gonsalves? Would anyone like a kitty?" He squirms around in his chair. He's so big, the desk moves too. "Our cat just had kittens."

Miss Gonsalves smiles at him. "Everyone get out your geography projects," she says.

*

We're doing maps of our own. There's a complicated list of things to put on the map: schools, churches, airports, train tracks, power lines. Coordinates, plotting, compass points.

I love maps. When we go traveling, I'm always in charge of the route. I love knowing exactly where we are, being able to point to a dot or a line on the map and say *I'm here!* Even better to be able to draw the map – to control the landscape, to draw the dot or the line in the first place.

In another life, I'd be an explorer.

"Psst, Jane," whispers Patti, turning around in her chair. Her eyes are round; her eyebrows go down. "Where's Northeast?"

Hard to answer that.

"Halfway between North and East," I whisper back.

"Huh? I mean, on my map."

Sunnyside School doesn't have a proper cafeteria, so we all eat lunch in our classrooms. Today it's – you guessed it – tuna sandwiches. Also an apple, some licorice, and grape juice to drink. Bill calls his grape juice grog.

I shouldn't complain about Mom's lunch-making. She hasn't had much practice. And the grog isn't bad.

Patti usually sits with me at lunch, but not today. She's over on the far side of the room, next to Brad. Why does this bug me? I don't know, but it does.

Essa and Justin sit ahead of me. She wriggles when she speaks to him – I think she likes him. He finishes a bite, wipes his mouth, and turns around.

"What do *you* think of my shirt, Jane?"

"Very nice." Not, you understand, that I care a whole lot. Justin wears a different shirt every day. This one is a bright green color. He looks like he's wearing a billiard table.

"Know what that is?" he asks, holding out his sleeve.

"A button?"

"Silly!" says Essa. "Of course it's a button."

"See what it's made of?" says Justin. "My mom and I were quite excited when we found it. See – real mother-of-pearl."

"It's beautiful," I say. "Truly beautiful."

Justin blushes like a doll, with a small red dot on each cheek.

Library is right after lunch on Wednesdays. I take one look at the wide-open rectangular floor space between the bookshelves, and get an idea. I whisper my idea to Miss Gonsalves, who says she'll ask the librarian. Miss Sucrete agrees at once. She's a good sort.

"Go right ahead," she says. "I'll close the doors to the rest of the school."

And so we have an impromptu *Nutcracker* rehearsal during our library period.

Miss Gonsalves waves us into position. She has beautiful hands. Long slender fingers like the branches of a willow tree. "Jane, we missed you yesterday after school," she says. "We had no one to tell us what to do."

Michael laughs, of course.

"And Brad, our star: you too were missed. Eh, Patti?"

Patti blushes.

Miss Gonsalves nods to me, and makes the *after you* gesture. I open my notebook.

"We'll do the scene after Godfather Stahlbaum comes down from the clock. The doll comes to life, and the mice appear from all over. Okay? Michael, in position: say, on top of that chair. Patti, right where you are; Brad kneeling beside you. The rest of the class, in the wings, waiting. Remember your dance steps."

This is a tricky section. Patti's doll turns into a real life-sized nutcracker. The mice attack. The toys defend. Hard to direct all this. I have to pay attention to lines; also to the flow of action across the stage. Before the battle begins, there's a dance. Essa and Justin worked it out. They take dance classes together.

I clap my hands. Everyone looks over. "Brad, you know what to do. Patti, your first line is 'Good gracious!' And . . . action!"

Brad is at Patti's feet (he'll be under a table when we get onstage). He stretches out his arms, as if waking up, and then climbs to his feet. Not gracefully, though. He's a nutcracker, a stiff-jointed mechanical thing. Brad is actually quite good. He gets into the part more than the other actors.

Miss Gonsalves can't play because there's no piano, but she hums, and moves her hands in time to the humming.

Patti puts her hand to her mouth – a lifelike gesture, this one, because she's very conscious of her braces. She stares at Brad, then away again. I hope she's confused because Maria is confused, and not because she doesn't know her lines. She'd better know her lines with the performance less than a week away. She smiles at Brad.

"Good . . . gracious. How can this be?
Nutcracker looks so strange to me!
A minute ago he was so small.
Now he'd crack open a bowling ball!"

Jiri laughs. He always laughs at this line. When he gets a joke, it stays got.

Brad bows stiffly to Patti. She smiles back, and brushes her blonde bangs away from her face. Another very Patti gesture.

Miss Gonsalves is wearing red today – a sweater and skirt combination, with a bright yellow shirt and a rope of pearls. "Great!" she calls out. "Nice chemistry, you two."

The dance sequence starts with the appearance of the evil Mouse King, who jumps out from behind the clock with the line:

"Woe to happiness and joys.
Woe to little girls and boys.
Woe, oh woe, to all their toys."

Then Maria shrieks and, on her shriek, the rest of the mice come running out of hiding places in the walls. They attack the toys, who retreat sideways: left-right-left-right. Essa calls it a grapevine. The toys attack back, and the mice retreat in another grapevine. Then the Nutcracker breaks his sword, and the mice come charging back. Maria throws her shoe, scattering the vermin. One of them bites her on the arm, and she faints.

The sequence starts well today. Justin stands beside me, frowning at the dancers. "Left, no *left*, you stupid cow!" he mutters. I don't know who he means – to my eyes, the dance looks pretty good.

At the height of the battle, when the Nutcracker has broken his sword (today, a ruler), Michael shouts, "Hey, look at that!" He points past me. The dancing toys turn to look. One of them trips. Justin groans, then turns to look himself.

"Wow!" he says.

The first dolly goes past me. Dolly, not doll. A two-wheeled dolly loaded with big cardboard boxes – the kind TV sets come in. Another dolly is coming through the library door. And another.

Crisply shaved strong men in blue winter overalls, with flapped caps on their heads and gloves on their hands, push the dollies. Principal Gordon comes in with the last one. He wears a red sweatshirt on his round belly and a pleased expression on his round baby face. He rubs his hands together. "Put them over there for now," he tells the strong men, pointing at our stage area.

Them – computers. In their boxes.

"It's the surprise!" squeaks Essa. "Remember the announcement this morning."

"Cool!" says Michael.

Gordon beams at us. He explains that the Board of Education offered our school a deal on some used computers.

"How many?" asks Michael.

"Used?" says Justin. "Used by whom?"

The men stack the computers on the floor, at the far side of the library. The boxes are folded at the top, not sealed. These are, after all, used computers. Box after box, all marked MONITOR. Then box after box, all marked TOWER. Then box after box, all marked PRINTER. They have a compulsive power. I feel it myself. I'm upset that our rehearsal has been interrupted – yet again – but I still find myself staring, counting the boxes.

So much power. So much knowledge. It's easy to understand the pull of the computer. Thirty towers – enough data in those boxes to run the whole country.

"Can you sign for these, sir?" asks the man with the first dolly. He reaches into his pocket for a bill. Yet another dolly wheels through the door. The boxes are all marked KEYBOARD ETC. The man in charge of it has no hat or gloves. He shivers.

Mr. Gordon takes the bill. The shivering guy trips on something. His dolly flips over, and the boxes go flying at us. "Sorry," he calls out.

"Help!" cries Patti. "Help!" The top box is open, and the contents are pouring out on her.

"Sorry, there!"

"Ouch!" cries Patti.

"Careful, there, Curly!" calls the guy in charge.

"I tripped," says Curly. "It's these new safety boots."

"Well, watch where you're going. Here, little girl, how are you?"

"I'm hurt!" She is too. Her arm is bleeding, from a sharp edge somewhere. Justin, beside her, seems very concerned with his shirt. He checks the sleeve for rips.

No keyboards in this box. It was full of etceteras. You know the kind of etceteras they mean: speakers, connectors, surge protectors, mouse pads – and the pointing, clicking animals that roll on them.

That's right. Patti, our heroine from long ago, has been attacked by a horde of modern-day mice.

7

Mom Is Crying

"Mom, I'm going to David's. Okay?"

Before Mom can reply, Bill's back out the front door. The knapsack on the floor in the hall is the only indication that he was ever in the house at all.

Mom and Bernie are in the family room. Mom is in the big chair. Bernie is bouncing on the couch. He says hi to me, and keeps on bouncing. Is Mom sleeping? I can't tell.

"It's not fair," I say. "They delivered some new computers right in the middle of our library period. We didn't even get a chance to finish our scene in *The Nutcracker*."

Bernie bounces up and down, talking to himself. "Once upon a time," I hear.

"At least Brad is healthy. But there's something going on with Patti. She doesn't want to talk to me. I think she likes Brad. I don't like him. He's too . . ."

I don't know what he's too. He smiles at me, and his smile is nice. When I tell him and Patti to move

55

downstage, he says sure. Patti doesn't. She sulks and pouts, as if this is the stupidest idea in the world. Or she asks Miss Gonsalves if my idea is any good. And Miss Gonsalves, bless her, says *Jane is the director. Better do what she says.* And Patti pouts, and moves slowly downstage.

She used to be my best friend. I don't like to tell her what to do, but the play is better if I do it my way. It's hard being the boss.

Upstairs I can hear coughing. "How's Daddy?" I ask Mom.

She doesn't answer.

"The doctor was here," says Bernie. "Daddy is taking a whole bunch of pills. I saw them." He holds out two hands with eight spread fingers. "This many pills," he says. His eyes are wide.

"Wow."

"Mommy cried," he confides, whispering.

"Oh." I go over to her, and stroke her arm. She turns her head and smiles without opening her eyes.

"When did you cry?" I ask. She doesn't answer.

"I spilled the juice on her computer," says Bernie. "And there was a big spark, and the lights went out."

"Oh."

"Mommy went down to the basement, and the lights came back on, but the furnace wouldn't start. Mommy tried and tried, but she couldn't start it."

"Oh."

"That's when she started to cry. The furnace man came. He let me help him. He had a lot of tools. When I dropped one, it made a big noise."

"Oh."

"Mommy cried some more. Then she got a call from work, and I had a nap. I wasn't tired, but I had to have a nap anyway. Would you read me a story, Jane?" he asks.

"Sure." I have math homework, but I don't feel like rushing to do it. It's all about patterns. You know: *what number comes next in this sequence?* Somehow the numbers I choose are not the same ones as the textbook. "Sure, Bernie."

We're halfway through a story about a little baby named Bun Bun, when Bill comes back from David's house.

"What's for dinner?" he asks, as he comes in the front door. Even before the front door closes, in fact.

Dinner. Good idea. I'm hungry. The picture in the story shows baby Bun Bun sitting on top of a birthday cake. Bernie is staring at the picture and licking his lips.

Mom's asleep in her chair. She wakes up. "Dinner," she groans. "Dinner."

The pizza place is on speed dial, right under the pharmacy. Mom gets through and then pauses with the phone in her hand. "What do we usually get?" she asks.

I stare at her. How can she not know? "Double cheese, pepperoni, and mushrooms for Bill and me, Hawaiian for you and Dad, and plain cheese for Bernie."

"Okay."

"Wait," says Bill. "I want to try one without the pepperoni this time."

I stare at him now. Mr. Impulsive. "Okay," I say. "I can take it. How about bacon instead? Or sausage?"

He shakes his head. "No bacon," he says.

"Sausage?"

"Just cheese and vegetables."

"No meat? What kind of weak pizza is that?"

"Weak? Extra onions," he says, staring at me like a challenge. Bill and I can be competitive about some things. About all things, actually. "And anchovies."

"Extra anchovies," I say.

"Okay, okay. And I bet I can eat more than you."

"Oh, yeah?"

Mom waves her hand, telling us to be quiet. She gives the order and hangs up.

"What is Hawaiian, anyway?" she asks.

"Ham and pineapple," I say.

"You're kidding. Who'd want to eat that?"

"You do. You eat it all the time. Don't you remember?"

She shakes her head. "I don't usually pay attention," she says. "Besides, your father eats most of it."

After dinner we all troop up to the third floor. We stand on the stairs outside the office and talk to Dad. He sounds weak.

"Are you really taking eight pills?" I ask.

"I don't know," he says. "Whole bunch, anyway."

"Are you better?" asks Bernie. "Mommy can't look after us."

"Hey!" says Mom. She's frowning.

"But that's what the furnace man said."

"He said *you* needed looking after, Bernie. That's not quite the same thing."

"I can help," says Bill. "I'm practically a man."

I elbow him in the ribs.

"I am," he says.

"You're eleven," I say.

"David is already studying to be a man. He told me all about it. When he's thirteen he'll be a man."

"Well, I'm thirteen," I say. "I guess I'm a woman already."

He elbows me in the ribs.

"Stop it!" says Dad. It's scary, hearing him say stop it, which he only does thirty times a day, in a voice that doesn't belong to him. It's like his normal voice strained through a sieve, taking out all the strength and humor.

Like an old man's. He starts to cough. *Ack ack ack ack ack ack.*

"We miss you, Dad," I say.

"Me, too," he whispers.

I wake up late at night. Not because of bowling from next door. I hear the sound no kid likes to hear. Mom is crying.

I'm scared. The whole idea of your mom crying is a scary idea. I'm the one who should be crying. Or Bill or Bernie. Mom's the one who should be saying *there, there.* I'm scared to go to her bedroom and say *there, there.* Scared I'll start crying too. I want to pull the covers over my head and go back to sleep, but I can't. I sit up in my bed and listen.

It's 12:30 by my clock. Apart from Mom, the house is quiet. She's not bawling her eyes out or anything, just weeping. The sound of her weeping trickles down the hall toward me, like water trickling out of the bath.

"Can't," she says.

She's talking. I get up and tiptoe to my bedroom door. Is she talking to Dad?

"Work calling me all the time, and I can't help them. I don't know how to run a house. I can't cook, and I can't do laundry, and Alex is so sick. I'm scared," she says.

My mom. Scared. I'm used to her being busy and far away. I'm used to her working hard, and being tired at the end of a long day, or at the end of a business trip. I'm used to her in her suit and makeup, looking calm and beautiful while Dad is screaming at us. *Now, Alex*, she'll say, *it's not fair to expect too much of them. They're only children.* Dad will gibber and throw his arms in the air the way you do when you score a touchdown. *Children? They're fiends, I tell you. Fiends from the pit!* We're already laughing, of course. Then he'll start laughing too, and the whole episode blows away.

Smart. That's my mom. Distant, too. I didn't know she was ever scared.

But she is. She's scared right now. And I don't know what to do for her. I take a step into the hall. I want to . . . I don't know what. But I want to see her. I know I'll feel better if I can just see her. I glide down the hall toward the big bedroom. The door is open.

Mom's voice gets louder. "I have a huge proposal that I have to get ready. They need me downtown. I can't help Alex. He needs rest. And I can't take another day here. Bernie said I can't look after them and he's right. I didn't do anything today except run up and down stairs, and call the furnace repair people. I fell asleep before dinner. I'm tired right now, and I can't sleep. I know it's a lot to ask of you, but I don't know who else to call."

She's pacing up and down in her robe. There are some papers on the bedside table. Her reading glasses are there too. The single light throws harsh shadows against the far wall. I stand still in the doorway. Her back is to me. She presses the phone against her ear. With her free hand she covers her eyes.

"Mother, I'm so scared," she says.

8

It's Grandma

I wake up because Bernie is bouncing on my bed.

"Jane, guess what?"

He lands on my leg. I sit up. "What time is it?"

"You'll never guess who's here."

I grab my clothes in one hand. "Who?"

He puts his face right up to my ear and whispers as hard as he can. I can't understand him, but I don't have to. I hear a familiar voice from downstairs.

"Jane Peeler? Get the shell out of bed, you lazybones! Breakfast!"

Sounds like it might be a cheery voice, but it isn't. It's scratchy and gruff, and there's a spitty kind of cough at the end of it. And the actual word isn't "shell." It rhymes with shell. I'm changing her words here because if I write down the words she actually says, I'll get in trouble.

"See," whispers Bernie.

I decide not to shower. I change really fast behind the bathroom door, and run downstairs to greet Grandmother Collins.

What can I say about her? Grandma is tall and skinny. She has bright eyes and frizzy hair and, generally, a cigarette hanging off the side of her mouth. Maybe because of the cigarette, her choice of words is often, um, grimy.

I used to think she was an awful old prune. She doesn't seem to like anyone very much. She spends a lot of time criticizing Dad and telling us kids to stop doing what we're doing. Then, this past summer, on our way to Auntie Vera's house in the Berkshires with a detour to Schenectady, I got to know Grandma better. And I found that I was wrong about her. Sure she's cranky and mean, but underneath her scaly exterior she has a heart of – no, I can't say that. Not gold. Not even silver. She does have a heart, though. She said a couple of nice things about me before we came back home.

She lives across the city, and we don't see her very often. None of us seems to mind very much.

She's in the kitchen now, long-fingered hands on her skinny hips. Cigarette pointing up, mouth turned down.

"About time," she says to me. A friendly greeting from Grandma. "Now, hurry up. You, too, Bernard. William is already finished his breakfast."

Bernie hangs behind me. He's scared of her.

The kitchen phone is on the wall beside the swinging door. The phone cord is usually twisted into knots. Now the phone is gone, and the cord stretches out the kitchen door. "Okay," says Mom's voice from the family room. "Okay, I'm on my way now. Bye, Fred. Yes, yes. See you soon. Bye." Mom comes into the kitchen carrying the phone.

She looks so much better than yesterday. You'd hardly guess she was up crying in the middle of the night. Suit, makeup, briefcase, coffee cup. She looks like her old self – her real self. She's even smiling.

"Hi, everyone," she says.

"Mommy!" Bernie rushes over to give her a hug.

She grabs his shoulders and keeps his sticky hands away from her skirt. "Hey, Bernie, how's my little baby?" she says. She puts him in his booster seat. "And now, children," picking up her briefcase, "I have an announcement."

We all look at her. Grandma coughs a couple of times, and spits into the sink. Mom frowns. "What?" says Grandma. Mom turns back at us.

"Jane, Bill, Bernie, your father is sick. He needs a lot of rest, so he can't look after you all, and the house, the way he usually does. I can't do all that and my regular job too, so I asked Grandma to help us. She'll be staying here until your father gets better."

She stops. I think we're supposed to cheer, or say great, or yippee, or something like that. We don't.

"I'm off to work now. Grandma will be here when you get back from school. She'll make dinner . . . what was that, Bill?"

"Nothing," says Bill. "Something stuck in my throat."

I smile. I know what he's thinking. Grandma is the world's worst cook. Seriously. If she were any worse, she'd be a mass poisoner. Dad's not very good, but he's a thousand times better than Grandma.

"And now I have to go. Bye-bye. I'll see you tonight."

Mom waves at us all, bends to kiss Bernie on the top of the head. "Thanks, Mother," she says, and heads off. Grandma doesn't say anything.

Bill is dressed, no missing pieces. There's an empty cereal bowl on the table. "Where's the hard tack?" I ask him.

"I don't eat tack all the time," he says. "David's family never do." He makes for the door.

Grandma blocks his way. "Put your bowl in the sink," she says. "I'm your grandmother, not your servant."

"But Dad –"

"Your father spoils you, and look where it got him," says Grandma. "Put the ham bowl in the sink. Okay?"

"Okay," mutters Bill.

"When did you get here, Grandma?" I ask. I meant to say how nice it was to see her, but somehow the words don't come out.

"Never mind when I got here," she says. "Just eat." She points to some clean bowls and spoons on the table, and a box of cold cereal. The little rounded spoon is there. It's our favorite. I can't believe Bill didn't grab it.

"I don't like that kind of cereal," I say.

"Tough," says Grandma.

Bernie turns around in his booster seat high chair to stare at her with wide eyes. His little hand creeps toward his mouth. I hope he's not going to cry.

"Here, Bernie," I say. I hand him the best spoon.

Grandma takes a deep drag on her cigarette. I wait and wait for the smoke to come out.

★

67

It's 10:00 and I'm in the school office, handing in the day's attendance sheet. Mrs. Winter is on the phone. She takes the sheet without looking at me. The principal's room is across the hall. He's sitting at his desk. "Can I see you for a moment, sir?" I ask.

He waves me in. There's a line of dark spots on the floor in front of his room. Is he the one in the marking shoes? I check them out when he comes around his desk.

"Hello, there." He raises a thick dark eyebrow. Then he puts it down, as if it's too heavy to lift up for long. "Is this about your class attendance?"

"No, sir. It's about rehearsals for *The Nutcracker*."

"Ah, *The Nutcracker*. I hear great things about that from Miss Gonsalves. You wrote the poems, I understand. Well done, um. . . ." He's forgotten my name.

"Jane Peeler, sir. Thank you, sir."

"You can call me Gordon."

"Yes, uh, Mr., uh, I mean, Gordon."

"Mr. Gordon is okay, too."

There's blue carpeting in the room. I can't tell if the principal's brown loafers are making marks or not. I go straight into my speech.

"We need to use the gym tonight for our rehearsals. Tomorrow night, too."

Gordon blinks. "Didn't you just have a rehearsal there the other night?"

"No, sir. We were supposed to, but I had to go to the hospital."

"Oh, yes. I remember now." He retreats back behind the desk and puts his hands in his pants pockets. He's wearing a sweatshirt with a soccer logo on the sleeve. He looks like an overage kid. He jigs from foot to foot. "You're sure you're not sick?"

"Yes, sir. I'm fine."

"That's good. Your brother seems to be all right. I saw him in the hallway before school."

"He's fine, too."

"A nice boy, your brother. Wished me a happy Chanukah."

"Yes, I bet he did."

"Now, um, Jane . . . about tonight . . ."

"We need the rehearsal, sir. Badly. The show is on Tuesday and we haven't had a chance to act onstage yet. Not at all. Didn't Miss Gonsalves explain?"

I wish she were here with me. She isn't even at school today. The substitute teacher is approximately three million years old. She thinks computers are newfangled. Also calculators and electric pencil sharpeners. *In my day we did things for ourselves*, she says. I'll bet she thinks the wheel is newfangled. *In my day we dragged stuff around.* Her jaw opens and shuts with a snap, like a spring-loaded box lid.

Miss Gonsalves promised she'd be back for the rehearsal tonight. I'll be glad to see her – there's so much to do.

The phone rings.

"About tonight," I say.

69

Gordon pauses with his hand on the receiver. He puffs his cheeks out at me. His eyebrows lumber up and down his face. "Tonight there's a basketball practice. The boys' team has a game next week."

"What? But Miss Gonsalves –"

"Mr. Gebohm reserved the gym. If you want it, you'll have to talk to him."

He picks up the phone. "Hello? Yes, Gordon Gordon here."

I don't leave. "What about tomorrow?"

He stares at me with the phone at his ear. "What's that?" he says.

"We get the gym tomorrow," I say. "Friday. For our rehearsal."

"What? Yes, yes, all right," he says.

"Thank you," I say, and walk out, thinking about Mr. Gebohm.

"My life is falling apart," I say to Patti at lunch recess. She's dressed up today. Her best shirt, hair in a beautiful – well, a carefully combed – style, all up and wrapped around her head, with little clips in a circle. No hat, even for outside recess. A hat would disarrange the hairstyle. She looks like she's ready to go synchronized swimming, or do battle with Jabba the Hutt.

"*Mmm hmm*," she says, looking over my shoulder. We're standing in the grade 7 section of the playground, near the school but not near the doors. We always stand here.

"My dad is really sick, so he's upstairs and no one can go near him. Mom has to work, so we're being looked after by my grandmother – the original dragon lady," I say.

"*Mmm hmm?*"

"Yes. She smokes like a chimney, swears worse than Michael. She's really bossy."

"There he is. Hi, Brad!" Patti hasn't been listening to me.

Brad smiles and comes over. His leather jacket is unzipped, exposing a sweatshirt with the picture of an album cover. The edges of the jacket hang over the first part of the group's name. I can see the second part: IMP IZKET. Brad waggles his eyebrows at Patti, who simpers and sucks her braces. I think she even blushes.

"Guess what, girls? I saw our supply teacher in the parking lot."

"She drives a car?" I can't believe it. "You sure it wasn't a horse and buggy?"

He smiles uncertainly. "Horse and buggy?"

"Don't mind Jane," says Patti. "What do you want to do now, Braddie?"

Braddie? Braddie?

The playground monitor is a ginger-mustached man, with a chest like a barrel and long bare hands that stick out of the bottom of his sleeves like pitchforks. His eyes glitter behind little glasses. Mr. Gebohm.

How can I convince him to let us have the gym tonight?

Mr. Gebohm is the gym teacher and coach. He's new this year. I don't know him very well, and don't like what I know. He's a hard man. His expression is hard. His heart is hard. Even the *G* at the front of his name is hard.

I walk up to him with my second-best smile. "Mr. Gebohm? I have a favor to ask you."

"Who are you?" he asks. "You don't play basketball." He turns away from me and scans the playground.

I smile harder. "Jane Peeler. Actually, it's about the gym that I want to talk to you."

"Gym?"

"Yes. I wonder if –"

"What Do You Think You're Doing?" When Mr. Gebohm yells, he sounds like an advertising slogan. Every word counts. He hurries toward a knot of little kids. I follow.

"Hey, Jane," calls Michael from the climbing bars. "Watch this!"

Why do I turn to watch? I don't like Michael. I don't like him when he's being his normal loud-mouthed self. I don't see any improvement when he's doing pull-ups on the climbing bars.

"You Think You're Going To Be Popular? You Think She Likes That?" Mr. Gebohm is yelling at Jiri.

There's a ring of little kids, grade ones and kinder-gartners, surrounding Jiri. There usually is. He gets along with them. In a way they're all of an age.

"Huh?" says Jiri. He's giving a little girl a ride on his back. He's smiling and panting earnestly, running up and down. She's pulling his hair and telling him to go faster.

Mr. Gebohm lowers his voice. "Did you hear me, big guy? I asked if you thought she liked it."

Jiri takes a second to work it out. "Uh-huh," he says.

"'Uh-huh.' What Kind Of Answer Is That?" He reaches his pitchfork hands toward the little girl, tries to pluck her off of Jiri's back. She clings like a scab.

I want to tell Mr. Gebohm to stop bothering Jiri. But I can't. I don't want to make him mad at me. He'll never give up the gym if he's mad at me. I look around for help. Brad is watching the whole scene. I wave. He turns away.

"Are You Stupid, Kid? Is That It? You Are, Aren't You? You're Just Stupid."

"Stop that!" I say.

The words pop out of me like sweat. I can't help them. I can't stand the idea of Mr. Gebohm calling Jiri stupid.

Startled, he turns to me. "You?"

I open my mouth, when I hear a familiar voice from the climber.

"Take that!" it says. Next thing I know, a snowball hits Mr. Gebohm right in the back of the head.

No snowballs are allowed on our school yard. None at all. I don't know what they're afraid of – little kids getting hurt, probably. I bet they aren't afraid of gym teachers getting hit.

He whirls around. "Who Did That?" he shouts. His eyes are slits behind his glasses. The snowball is melting down the back of his neck. I bet it's melting fast – his neck is so hot. He's so mad, there's steam coming off him.

"Oh, sorry, sir," calls Michael, from the climber, with a smile on his face. "I didn't mean to hit you. I was aiming . . . um . . . somewhere else."

I relax. I don't mind Michael getting in trouble. He's used to it, and he can handle it.

Jiri stands still with the little girl on his back. "*Do* you like this?" he asks, twisting around to look up at her. He has whiskers – the only one in grade 7.

The girl shrieks and pulls his hair. "Go, Jiri, go," she cries. He trots off.

Mr. Gebohm crooks his hand at Michael. "Come Here, You!" he says.

I think about asking him the favor, but now doesn't seem like the right time. I turn back to the school. Patti has Brad in a headlock. He doesn't seem to mind.

9

Go Boom

First class after lunch is math. Our three-million-year-old supply teacher reads a question from the textbook in her ancient, reedy voice, and then looks up and says: "So, what's the answer?" The question is one of those word problems, where two trains are rushing away from each other at different speeds, and Agatha is three times as old as Gerald will be in two years, and the white box weighs more than black box but only half as much as the red box.

"If one mousetrap catches one mouse every day," she reads, slowly, "and two mousetraps catch four mice, and three traps catch nine mice, and four traps get sixteen mice, then how many traps will be needed to catch twenty-five mice?"

Jiri drops one of his letter blocks. He uses them to spell out the words he's practicing. GOAT BOAT ROAD are some of them this week. I know this because I helped him yesterday. In our class the quick learners

75

get to help the slow learners. I'm usually one of the quickest, and Jiri is always the slowest.

"Pick that up," says the teacher. "In *my* day we didn't get colored blocks to play with, and if we did, we wouldn't have dropped them. What's your name?"

"Me?" says Jiri, bending quickly to pick up the block. "My name is Jiri Holocek my family comes from Prague that is in Europe." He says this all in one breath, the way he always says it. He has a big smile. "Pleased to meet you," he says.

She frowns. "Did you hear the question, Jiri? How many traps would it take to catch twenty-five mice?"

I look around the class and see my own embarrassment reflected in other people's faces. I wish Michael were here to help, but he's still in the principal's office for throwing snowballs. "Uh, it's not fair to ask Jiri that question," I say at last.

She peers at me. "And why not? In *my* day teachers could ask students questions. They were even encouraged to do it."

"Uh, Jiri is. . . ." All right, I don't know how to put it. "He's . . ."

"No problem, Jane," says Jiri. "I can answer the question."

I squirm uncomfortably. "But . . ." I begin, and then stop.

I poke Patti, sitting in front of me. She shrugs her shoulders and doesn't turn around. Justin fiddles with the zipper at the top of his sweater. Brad is sharpening his pencil, collecting the shavings in a neat pile on the corner of his desk.

"How many traps then, Jiri?" asks the teacher.

Jiri smiles. His glasses are filthy. His whiskers shine. "One," he says.

"Wrong, wrong, wrong," she sighs, shaking her head. "Standards, standards. Today's standards are nowhere near what they were in *my* day. Why, the next number in sequence –"

"Of course, you would need almost a month," says Jiri.

"What?" she gasps. "What was that?"

"You said that one mousetrap catches one mouse a day," says Jiri, patiently. "So that in twenty-five days you would catch twenty-five mice, with one mouse-trap. Do you see?"

"But . . . but I meant. . . ." She's having trouble getting his thoughts in order.

Silence. I can't help it. I laugh.

I'm not alone. Around the room smiles are popping out, shyly, like early crocuses. Zillah, from in front of Michael's empty desk, taps her fingertips together. Her black nails are very striking.

The bell rings for gym. The teacher's jaw closes with a snap.

"Line Up For Dodgeball!" shouts Mr. Gebohm. "Along the wall."

Mr. Gebohm has changed into gray gym shorts – no, what I mean is, he's changed his clothes. He looks more natural than in the long pants he wore on the playground at lunchtime. These are his real work clothes.

"You, there," he says, glaring at Michael, back from the principal's office with a note to take home, "go to the other side of the gym."

Mr. Gebohm can talk with the whistle in his mouth. All gym teachers can. "You, too," he calls to Justin.

Michael stalks away. Justin glides after him, his pants swishing around his skinny hips.

"You, too," says Mr. Gebohm, pointing farther down, "and you, and you." He points to every second or third person, separating us into two teams.

"Okay! Go!" he says, whipping the ball at Justin. It flies like a big round white bullet, and hits him on the knee.

"You're Out!" cries Mr. Gebohm. Justin hobbles to the sidelines, grimacing. "Come On!"

Michael picks up the ball and throws it, almost as hard as the teacher. At whom does he aim? Why, me of course. I think Michael must hate me particularly – he's always picking on me. I don't know why – I'm not mean to him. I don't make fun, or anything. I picked him to be Godfather Stahlbaum in the play. Most of the time I try to be nice to him. And not just because he's a bully, the way you'd be nice to a Mafia don who happened to be in your homeroom.

Anyway, I stand still, like a deer in the headlights, only I'm not as big – say, a woodchuck in the head-lights, while the ball travels toward my face at the speed of light, looming bigger and bigger, blocking out the rest of the world.

Then Brad steps in front of me and tries to catch the ball. He misses. He's out. "Sorry, Jane," he says.

I smile at him – a nice guy. "Thanks for saving me," I say.

"Got you, Brad!" cries Michael. "Brad the weenie!"

Patti's face is red. She picks up the bouncing ball and hurls it at Michael. It goes way high, hits the bas-ketball backboard, and actually bounces in.

We all laugh and cheer. "Good shot!" I call to her.

She stares at me. Her eyes are narrow. My best friend – what's wrong with her?

Michael and Jiri are the two biggest and strongest boys in the class, and they're on opposite teams. Michael throws the ball really hard, but Jiri always seems to hold back.

"Harder!" his team shouts at him. "Throw it harder, Jiri."

What he can do is catch the ball. In dodgeball, if you catch the other team's throw before it bounces, the thrower is out. Jiri has the softest hands. He has trouble hitting anyone else with the ball because he doesn't throw very hard, but he gets lots of people out because he catches their throws.

Another thing he can do is dodge. I don't know how. He's big and a bit bulky, but he sideslips effort-lessly. Time and again I'm sure someone is going to nail him, but at the last second he shuffles to one side and the ball sails past. He's the size of a moose, but he swoops like a bird, out of the way of oncom-ing trouble.

It helps that Michael is not throwing at him. Michael prefers to pick the other members of the team. One by one, we all fall to him.

When I am hit, fairly early, I sit on the end of the bench. Brad comes over to sit down.

"Hey, thanks again," I say.

Then Patti gets hit, and runs to sit beside me. "Hi, there!" I say, glad to see that she's got over being mad. But she's not even talking to me. Head turned, she has something to say to Brad.

Only two people left. Michael on one side, and Jiri on the other. Mr. Gebohm is smiling around the whistle in his mouth, and rubbing his hands together. I realize, now, that this is what he wanted. The two boys are opponents. He didn't like Michael sticking up for Jiri on the playground. "Come on, boys. Throw hard now. Next one's the winner."

Jiri has the ball. He frowns, and puts the ball down. "A tie," he says.

"No!" shouts Mr. Gebohm. "I Want One Of You To Get It!"

Jiri frowns at him. "Please?"

"Come On!" Mr. Gebohm mimes throwing the ball. "Throw, Stupid!"

Jiri shrugs, and aims a gentle toss at Michael, who doesn't even try to catch it. He lets it roll to him, then in one motion picks the ball up and whips it as hard as he can – at Mr. Gebohm.

It hits him right in the cheek. His glasses go flying. His whole head snaps back. There's a muffled *tweet* from his whistle – the last sound a canary would make on its way into the cat's mouth – and the teacher falls over, hitting the gym floor.

"Gebohm go boom!" says Michael.

Jiri frowns, then he gets the joke. He opens his mouth wide, and laughs and laughs. Mr. Gebohm is sitting up now. The whistle dangles. "Gebohm go boom!" says Jiri.

I walk over to the teacher. "Can we rehearse our play in the gym after school today?" I ask. "Please, Mr. Gebohm."

He stares blankly up at me. "No," he says.

10

Happy to Be a Girl

And so we have another rehearsal in class. Miss Gonsalves arrives in good time and good spirits. She laughs when I tell her about meeting the principal, and trying to convince Mr. Gebohm.

"Wait until they hear my news," she says, opening her music.

"What news?"

"I'll tell you tomorrow. I won't know for sure until then."

Snow is falling when I get out of the rehearsal. I can hear the scrape of shovels on the sidewalks – a sound muted by the falling snow. Bill is busy on our front walk. He isn't the only one. His friend David is there too. A big kid, David. Bigger than Bill – than me, come to that. He looks like a bear in his winter coat, and hat with the earflaps dangling.

"About time," says Bill. "Hurry and help us, Jane. She won't let us in until the walk is cleared."

"What do you mean, she? She, who?"

"Who do you think – Grandma."

"Oh."

"Your grandmother reminds me of my aunt," says David. "Very strict."

"Strict?" says Bill. "She's crazy." Then he says something I don't understand. Sounds like "sugar." "Is that right?" he asks David.

David smiles. "That's right," he says, bending to lift another shovelful of snow.

The back door of the house opens onto a mudroom. Hooks for coats, a tray for boots, a box for recycled papers. We hang up our coats.

The smell from the kitchen is powerful. A strong and sweet smell, like burning sugar. Bill and I share a glance. Grandma is probably the world's worst cook. Did you ever hear of the Donner party? They were in the Rocky Mountains and they ended up eating each other. Maybe I'd rather go to one of Grandma's dinners than the Donner party – but it would be a tough choice.

"Is the walk done?" yells Grandma from the kitchen. "And is your hairy friend here?"

"The walk's done, Grandma," I say.

"David isn't hairy," says Bill. "And he's gone home."

"Well, hang up your coats!" Grandma coughs loud and long, and spits in the sink.

Yuck.

I run upstairs to check on Dad. He's asleep. Back down on the second floor, I notice Bernie's bed has been rolled into Bill's room. The door to Bernie's room is closed. Grandma is moving in. Am I ever glad I'm a girl. No way they're going to put Bernie in with me.

Bill's sitting on his bed. "Ha-ha," I say from the doorway. "Got yourself a roomie, hey?" Not serious teasing, you understand. Just enough to let him know that I'm doing better than he is.

Bill ignores the teasing. "Do you think David's hairy?" he asks.

"He sure is," I say. "And messy too."

"Shut up."

Back in the kitchen, the smell is stronger than ever. It's coming from the oven. I don't know what it is. Bernie is kneeling on a chair. He has the games box out on the kitchen table, and he's trying to get Grandma to play something.

He holds up the dominoes. "Do you want to –"

"No," says Grandma.

"Oh. Well, what about –"

"No." Grandma opens the oven door. Heat shimmer blurs the atmosphere.

Bernie opens a pack of cards. "What abou –"

"No."

"Well, what *do* you want to do?"

She closes the oven door, stares over at him. "You wouldn't believe me."

"I'll play with you, Bernie," I say.

He smiles, fans the playing cards in his two hands. "Pick a card," he says.

I take a card. Bernie gets off the chair and walks away. "Hey, Bernie!" He keeps walking. I'm left holding the card. Bernie goes upstairs.

I thought the deck in his hands looked kind of thin.

"So, how's it going?" I ask Grandma. "Do you like my new earrings?" Two of them, high up on my left ear. Plain rings. I got them in time for Halloween. Dad didn't like the idea. Actually, "didn't like" puts it mildly.

Grandma shrugs at my earrings. "How's it going? I'll tell you how it's going. I'm living in a room with teddy bears on the wall," she says.

"Aren't they cute?"

"No."

"What's for dinner?" I ask.

There's smoke coming out of the oven now. Grandma whirls around. "Son of a ditch!" she yells, throwing open the oven door. She takes a pan out of the oven. In it is a smoking mass – or should I say, a smoking mess. I have no idea what she's cooking. Rounded, flatish, black things. Sandwiches? English muffins? Mini pizzas? Frisbees? Wagon wheels?

Grandma holds the pan over the sink, and starts scraping the black off the . . . things.

"What are *those*?" I ask.

"Pork chops," she says.

I don't say anything.

"Shut up," she growls, scraping. As the top black layer flakes off, I start to recognize them. It's like archaeology, I suppose. The trick is to see the meat underneath the coating of . . . of what?

"What's the stuff on top?"

"Marshmallow," she says.

Of course.

"Pork goes with sweet things," she says. "Applesauce, honey . . ."

"And marshmallow," I say.

Grandma puts down the pan, and stirs something cooking on the stove.

I don't ask what it is.

"Beans," she says, without looking around. "And brown sugar. You've had it before."

The front door opens. "Hello?" calls Mom. Her voice sounds tentative. She doesn't know what to expect. I run to the front hall.

"Mom!" cries Bernie from upstairs.

Mom has a funny expression on her face. "What's for dinner?" she says.

"You won't believe it," I whisper, peeking back over my shoulder. "Grandma is cooking pork chops with –"

"Marshmallow. That's it." Mom nods her head. "I recognize the smell."

"She's done this before?"

"Dinner!" calls Grandma.

Grandma finishes first, pushes her chair back, and opens her pack of cigarettes. Empty. She frowns at it, crumples it up, and tosses it onto her empty plate.

I swallow a small mouthful of dry burnt leather – that's what dinner tastes like.

"There's another pack of cigarettes in the bathroom," I say.

"I know," says Grandma. She doesn't move. Grandma has always smoked. Her apartment on the other side of the city has ashtrays and lighters on all the tables. One lighter is shaped like a gun. Last time we visited, Bill almost set Bernie's hair on fire.

"What's everyone staring at?" she says. "I don't *need* a cigarette. I'll wait."

"Good for you!" says Mom.

Grandma doesn't say anything.

"Smoking is bad for you," says Bill. He's not eating the pork chops, I notice. He's trying manfully – boyfully, anyway – with the beans.

87

"Why is smoking bad for you?" asks Bernie. He doesn't go to school yet, so he hasn't seen all the anti-smoking videos.

"Smoking turns your lungs all black," says Bill, "so that you can't breathe. You pant and fall down. And then your arteries get all hard, and you have a heart attack. And –"

"Boys," says Mom, "can we talk about something else, please?"

"No, no," says Grandma. "Keep going. Tell me more about how my body's falling apart. I love it." She coughs.

Mom's cell phone rings from inside her purse in the hall. She stands up. "Please excuse me, Mother, but I'm expecting an important call." She carries her plate to the counter. She hasn't eaten everything.

Grandma sniffs. "Important call," she says.

"What's Daddy getting for dinner?" I ask.

"Soup," she says. "Plain chicken soup out of a package. That's all he wants."

Lucky Dad. Packaged chicken soup sounds pretty good.

"Do you wish you had a cigarette now?" I ask Grandma.

"Yes," she says.

"And do you really like hearing about your body falling apart?" asks Bernie.

"No."

11

The Scariest Thing

The scariest thing happens to me that evening.

My favorite thing to wear in the universe is a fluffy oversize vest I bought on sale for fifteen dollars. Under the vest I like to wear a dark green button-down shirt from the Goodwill and what they call end-user pants – the kind with lots of ties and zippers. I can't find my vest or my end-users in my closet or dresser, or in the pile of dirty clothes that grows on the floor beside my bed. I haven't worn them in a few days. Did Dad wash them? I go down to the laundry room to check.

When I'm at the bottom of the basement stairs, I hear whispering behind and above me. The basement door shuts, leaving me in the dark.

"Very funny, Bill!" I call.

This isn't the scary bit. I can hear him and Bernie giggling, and I know the basement light is two steps in front of me. There's a long pull chain, dangling from the bare bulb in the ceiling. I walk forward in the dark and wave my arms about until I make contact with the string. I pull it, and everything jumps into focus.

Our basement is unfinished. There's a lot of exposed bricks and insulation and wires strung near the ceiling. A crib in the middle is filled with all kinds of junk we've outgrown. Washer, dryer, and laundry tub against one wall, with a pile of dirty laundry in front of them. Dresser against another wall – filled with more junk. Our old furnace crouches in the far corner, like a giant hunkered down for the winter, wheezing and grumbling. That's about all there is in the basement, except dust and spiders, and I don't mind either of them. And the single bulb with the pull chain.

I find my end-users in the pile of dirty clothes, and they're clean enough to wear. Good. I put them off to the side. I'm bent over again, hunting for my vest, when there's a flash, and the light goes out.

I freeze. It's really dark. And quiet.

Something moves away from me, rustling against things in the dark. "Bill, I can hear you!" I say.

The rustling stops.

"Hey!" I shout. No reply. "Hey!"

I turn around and reach for the pull chain, but I can't seem to find it. I flail around and lose a sense of where I am. You know how it is in the dark.

There's Bill again. I can hear him rustling ahead of me. Wait until I get my hands on him. I edge forward. And edge some more. And some more. And . . . .

It's taking me longer than I expect. I keep my hands out in front of me so I don't bump into anything.

Spiderwebs! Drat. I don't mind them when I can see them, but I hate brushing against them in the dark. I wipe my face, and keep going, slowly, slowly. . . .

Ah! The pull chain. What a relief! I pull it and – nothing happens. Maybe Bill didn't turn the light out. Does that mean I'm alone down here? "Bill?" I call, moving forward.

I bump into something with my knee. Ouch! I reach out and touch the laundry tub. I thought I was by the staircase, but I'm nowhere near it. I'm in the wrong part of the basement.

The rustling comes back. I freeze solid. In front of me is a wall. On the other side of the wall is Cisco's house. No way could Bill be there. In front of me is just a wall.

The noise is coming from there. From *inside* the wall. I scream.

Screaming is like pouring ketchup from a full bottle. It may be hard to start, but once you've started screaming, it all comes out in a rush. You usually end up with too much, noise covering everything, pooling in the middle of the plate, running off the sides, and you wish you'd kept your mouth shut.

I stagger backwards, screaming. I bump against something, trip, and end up by the stairs. I keep screaming and screaming.

★

A shaft of light, shining down on my dark world. Light from the kitchen. The door is open. Mom calls my name. I can't stop screaming. Mom runs downstairs.

I spend the rest of the evening in the family room. I try to tell Mom about the rustling noise, and she says *there, there,* and strokes my hair. That feels nice. Then she wraps a blanket around me and turns on the TV. She has work to do upstairs. Bernie bounces on the couch beside me. Ordinarily this would bother me, but tonight it's soothing. He's company.

I can't help wondering if it was Bill down in the basement all the time, scaring me. If it was, I'll kill him.

During a commercial I wander into the kitchen for a glass of juice. The basement door is open. I go over. I hear noise coming from the dark below.

"Hello?" I call. If it's Bill downstairs, I'll close the door and see how he likes it.

The basement light comes on. "Hello, yourself," calls Grandma.

I go down a couple of steps and peer into the basement. Grandma is standing on a chair, screwing in the lightbulb. "Can you hear a rustling noise down there?" I ask.

"You know, missy, I think I can." She steps down off the chair, pulls the chain so that the basement disappears in darkness.

I should do homework, but I can't bring myself to do it. I watch TV shows I don't care about, following images across the screen, not paying attention to the dialogue. Bernie stops bouncing, trots off. I hear him talking to Grandma. "Do you want to –"

"No," says Grandma.

12

"Humbug!"

I dream about going camping, which is strange because we don't camp. Not since the time two years ago when Bill, pretending to be a pioneer, insisted on chopping firewood. He swung hard, smashing the container of spaghetti sauce instead of the log he was aiming at. Then he swung again, knocking down the tent; and again, slicing a big hole in the canoe. Three strokes and we were out – no dinner, nowhere to sleep, and no way to move on. That incident ended Bill's attempt to live the pioneer life.

I wake up. There's the smell of smoke in my nostrils. Cigarette smoke. Strange, because no one in the household smokes – no, wait. I'm forgetting Grandma. I frown, and go back to sleep. I dream some more, this time about an outdoor bowling alley. There's a shoe rental, a vending machine selling potato chips, and a campfire. Someone a few lanes over is crying for help. There's a witch sitting around the campfire, roasting marshmallows. She cackles when the pins go down.

"Help!"

I sit up. It's Dad's voice.

"Hey! Help!"

I get out of bed. I don't hear anyone bowling. I look out in the hall.

"Help!"

I run to the stairs and peer up. "Oh, Dad!" He's in the corner of the stairs, where they turn on the way down from the third floor.

He's crouched in a ball. "I'm lost!" he says, in a small voice.

I run up the stairs and grab him by the hand. "Dad!"

"Helen?"

His hand is so hot, but he's shivering. It's very strange. "It's me, Dad. Jane."

"Jane?"

"Your daughter."

"I don't know where I am," he says.

"But you're home."

"I'm lost."

"No, you're not. You're found." I lead him up the steep stairs to the third floor, my poor lost dad. His face is covered in sweat. He can't stop shivering.

Mom is asleep in a chair beside the couch. The upstairs office is not like I remember it a few days ago. The computer table is pushed into the far corner, out of the way. The couch has sheets and blankets on it. They're all rumpled now. The desk is covered in pill

95

bottles and thermometers and washcloths. Mom startles awake as we come in.

"Alex," she says. A tone I'm not used to hearing. "Oh, dear, Alex, what are you doing?"

"I got lost," Dad whispers. His eyes are bright as stars. He lets Mom take charge of him, pushing him onto the couch, covering him up with blankets.

"What's wrong with Dad?" I ask.

"He's feverish. He isn't making a lot of sense," says Mom. She puts her hand on Dad's forehead, shakes her own head, and checks the clock on the desk. "Still two hours until his next pill," she says.

"Is he going to be all right?" As I'm talking, he falls back on the pillow and starts to snore.

Mom turns and smiles. Her lip trembles, though. "Course he is, honey. Course he is."

"Good."

"Now, get back to bed. It's really late."

"Night, Mom."

"Night, Jane."

On the second floor I can smell cigarette smoke. The lights are off in the family room and downstairs hall. Grandma's coming up to bed. I see the glowing red coal of the cigarette bobbing up the stairs ahead of her, like one of those guttering old candles that Ebenezer Scrooge would light himself to bed with. I don't know why Grandma makes me think of Ebenezer Scrooge – they've got nothing in common except that they both stay up late at night. And they're both grouchy old people with no one to care about them. Hardly anything in common.

"Humbug!" growls Grandma, when she sees me.

"What?"

"I said humbug. Do you have any humbugs? You know, those little striped mints. I usually keep some in my purse, but I'm all out of them."

"Sorry," I say.

She coughs a couple of times. "What are you staring at?" she rasps at me.

"Nothing."

"So I have a cigarette before bed. So what?"

She wears a pointy nightcap on her head. And her slippers are down at heel. And her nightie is big and wraps around her body. All she needs to complete the picture is the Ghost of Christmas Past, and Tiny Tim.

There's something moving in her hair. I peer at it in the glow of her cigarette.

"Why do you have a spider on you?" I ask.

"Where?" She swipes at it. I worry for the spider. I reach and take it off her. She shudders, looking at the spider in my hand. "Must have picked it up in the basement," she says.

"Quiet down there!" Mom calls from upstairs. "I have to leave early tomorrow."

"Sorry, Mom." I go to bed.

"*Hmph*," says Grandma. But she goes to bed too. The cigarette stays in her mouth.

"Where's the nearest hardware store?" Grandma asks at breakfast. She's dressed in a shapeless Grandma skirt and a big sweater with buttons.

"There's the Dominion Hardware store on Copernicus Street," I say. "Two blocks or so, next to the fruit store."

"That's where we get our Christmas tree," says Bernie.

"Uh-huh," says Grandma.

"When are we getting our Christmas tree?"

Grandma shrugs. "Soon, I guess, Bernard," she says.

"That's what Daddy always says."

I wonder what Grandma wants at the hardware store. Probably not humbugs.

Before leaving for school, I run upstairs to see how Dad is doing. He's sitting up, propped against a bunch of pillows. His eyes are open to slits. There's a cool cloth on his forehead. He looks weak.

"You were wandering around the house last night," I tell him. "You got lost on the stairs. Do you remember?"

He shakes his head.

"How are you feeling now?"

He shrugs. "Not too bad," he says.

I can hear footsteps on the stairs. Slow-moving footsteps, and labored breathing.

Dad's hand is still hot. I pat it. "Will you get better?"

He tries to smile. "Course I will," he says.

Grandma enters, breathing heavily. "Ham stairs," she says. "Three floors and no elevator. My hip feels like the *Hindenburg*. Time for your medicine," she says. She flops down in the chair to rest.

"Okay, Mother-in-law," says Dad.

Grandma takes a pill bottle from the desk, holds it a long way away from her and peers at the writing. "Two pills, with water," she mutters. She removes the lid and shakes out the pills. One of them drops on the floor. Grandma swears quietly. She stares at me. I go down on my hands and knees and hunt around on the floor under the couch. I find the pill, and hand it to her.

Getting my lunch from the fridge, I notice that the shelves are pretty empty. A single slice of baloney in the meat keeper. A wilting head of lettuce in the crisper. Some dried-up cheese. Three pickles floating belly-up in a jar of brine. "What's for lunch today, Grandma?" I ask cautiously.

"Cheese, lettuce, and ketchup sandwiches," says Grandma.

Bill and I laugh. "No, really," says Bill.

Grandma just looks at him.

13

Not Taking No for an Answer

End of the last period of the day, and my brother's class is leaving the gym. Through a crack in the stage curtain, I see his friend David – at least I assume it's David. He's the only one in the class who wears one of those beanies. The gym class leaves echoes of their shouts and giggles behind them, like a trail of audible litter.

Miss Gonsalves gave me the period off to prepare the stage for our first real rehearsal. Mr. March carried the tall chest of drawers back up from the basement. The big cardboard clock face had fallen off, so I stuck it back on. It's sitting upstage center, under the hanging backdrop. I'm making little crosses out of masking tape and sticking them to the stage floor. These crosses are called marks. The actors are supposed to end up standing on them after their big dance number. I check the chart Miss Gonsalves and I made a few days ago.

The gym class is gone. Time passes with a big broom, sweeping away the litter of noise. I finish taping down the crosses. I'm at the back of the stage now, hidden in darkness. The gymnasium is quiet. I can hear a whisper from across the room.

"So don't *you* think she's a bit too –"

"Uh-huh."

The whispered voices echo like cathedral bells. I know at once whose they are, and who they're talking about. It's Patti and Brad, and they're talking about me. Don't ask me how I know this, I just do. I'm not at all surprised to hear Patti's next line.

"Jane's my best friend, so I have to be nice."

"Uh-huh," says Brad.

"And, really, it's not her fault her dad's sick."

"Uh-huh."

"She can't help being a bit of a pill right now."

Hey. What's this?

"Uh-huh," says Brad again. A very slick talker.

"Funny, isn't it, that we both feel the same way about her. She just loves to give orders – and tell you that you're doing something wrong. *Talking too soft* – don't you hate it when she says that? Or, *too fast.* Or, *you're moving too awkwardly.* Or, *you're looking too bland.* What does that mean, anyway? Don't people like to look at me? Don't you like to look at me, Brad?"

There's a pause. I wonder if he's looking at her. My skin feels like a flashing light – now it's red, now it's not. Now it's red again.

"She doesn't tell *me* I talk too fast," says Brad.

"No, of course not. You have a beautiful speaking voice."

"And she doesn't say I move awkwardly."

"Oh, no. But . . . she did say you had to pay more attention to your cues. Remember? It was the rehearsal before last, and you were late coming in a couple of times when the Toy Soldier speaks to you. Remember? The rest of us were standing around, and Jane told you not to hold the whole company up."

I can hear them clearer than ever. They must be leaning against the side of the stage. I smile to myself.

Understand me, please. I'm mad and upset, and I feel betrayed. I haven't told too many people about Dad. I've known Patti since kindergarten. I guess she likes Brad, and is acting stupidly because of that. Her words are mean, and I feel hurt. *But*, it's also kind of funny. That's why I'm smiling. Patti is trying to get Brad to say he likes her, and he won't. Not yet, anyway. I'm hurt, but fascinated. It's like finding a huge pimple. You could forget about it, but you don't. You pull back your hair, and stare into the mirror at the big ugly red blotch.

Right now I should leave. I should go out the door at the back of the stage, and walk down the hall and come back in the gym by the regular door. They'd stop their whispering and say hi, and we could all talk together. I should do that. I shouldn't be listening. But I can't help myself.

"So, you're saying I was holding everyone up?" asks Brad.

"Oh, no."

"Slow on my cues? Did *you* feel I was letting the company down?"

"No, no, no. I'm saying that's what Jane said. Jane, not me."

"I wasn't slowing anyone down."

"No! Not at all. It was great. Wonderful timing. The way you, um, paused before your line was great. Very . . . dramatic."

"Paused?"

"I mean –"

"I didn't pause. I was right on my cue."

Now I'm not red anymore. In fact, I'm trying not to laugh. Poor Patti. She's making things worse with Brad. Maybe he really doesn't think much of her. Maybe he doesn't think I'm too bossy. Maybe he even, sort of, likes . . . me?

Oh, my. Now, I'm red again.

The bell rings. The door at the back of the gymnasium slams open. Michael's voice bounces around the gym like a rubber ball.

The place fills up with other students as they come in for the rehearsal. Miss Gonsalves will probably be along any minute. I creep back to the door at the back of the stage. I push the handle.

The door is locked from the other side.

Oh-oh.

I'm trapped on the stage. Now I can't sneak out and walk around and come in the main door, pretending that nothing has happened. But how can I walk out onstage? How am I going to face Brad and Patti? They'll know I was listening to their conversation. How can I do that?

"I wonder where Jane is?" asks Essa. "Have you seen her, Justin?"

"She wasn't at our last class," says Jiri.

Silence. Somebody – probably Michael – plays a few notes on the piano. Pretty soon they're going to be climbing all over the stage. Got to think fast.

"Have *you* seen her, Patti?" asks Essa.

"No. Brad and I . . . I mean we were the first ones here."

"She's been more worried about Brad," says Michael. "Ha-ha-ha."

I sneak back toward the door at the back of the stage. If only it wasn't locked! Or, if only I was outside, I could –

Wait a minute. They don't know the door is locked. And doors are for coming in as well as for going out. I've told everyone that, at rehearsal. *It's a door, Patti, don't stand in front of it.*

I grab my knapsack and rattle the handle of the door at the back of the stage. I make a lot of noise banging around, as if I was just coming in from the hallway. Then I walk past the curtain to the edge of the stage and peer down. Patti and Brad are standing next to each other. She has her hand on his arm. She looks up at me, then away again.

"Hi, everyone," I say. "Sorry I'm late." I pull open the curtain and walk across the front of the stage. "Welcome to the seventh grade production of *The Nutcracker*." I smile down at them all. "Let's get started."

"Shouldn't we wait for Miss Gonsalves?" asks Patti.

"She's coming," says Essa. "She wanted to talk to the principal about something."

"Then let's –"

A whistle blast cuts off my words. I stare across the gym floor at a big beefy man, with a whistle in his mouth and a clipboard in his hand. A ginger-haired man in sweatpants and a tight T-shirt, with little glasses that glitter in the harsh gym lighting.

Guess who?

He spits out his whistle. "Come On, You Guys!" he shouts. All the way across the room I can see the split veins and ruddy skin around his cheeks. Mr. Gebohm. Behind him the door to the locker room opens, and the first of the boys comes out. Tall skinny boys, with baggy shorts and vests, and expensive running shoes.

The boys' basketball team. I recognize the third or fourth boy out. He's the captain. Six feet tall – taller than my dad. He can dunk the ball. He doesn't look at us. None of the boys looks at us. They grab basketballs from the rack, and start dribbling around the court. The gym fills up with noise the way a bath fills up with hot water.

I don't know what to do. "Stop!" I shout as loud as I can, but it's like shouting at Niagara Falls. The bouncing noise continues. The boys are shooting layups.

The gym is ours! Gordon Gordon said so. That Gebohm is just a big bully. Where's Miss Gonsalves? The class is staring at me.

"Maybe we should go," says Brad. "Or else we'll . . . ." I can hardly hear him over the noise.

"It's *our* rehearsal," I say. "And we're having it here."

I'm not mad. I'm determined. I get that way sometimes. I'm beyond mad. I'm *going* to get my way. It has nothing to do with being angry. It's about not taking no for an answer. This is our practice period, and we are going to use the gym. No "or else." We are. Period.

I don't know how this is going to happen, but I know – *I know* – it will.

"Nobody move!" I call out to the cast, who are starting to pick up their gear.

I remember when I got my new earrings. This was around Halloween. Dad was working on Bernie's costume. I told him how much the earrings meant to me. He nodded sympathetically, but said I couldn't get them. "Sorry," he said.

"So, what can I do?" I asked.

He had safety pins in his mouth and his hands full of toilet paper because Bernie was going to be a mummy for Halloween. "I don't know what you can do," he said. "I've made my decision. It's no."

"But you said you were sorry. So you don't like the decision either."

"What?"

I opened my eyes wide. "You can always do something, if you want to. That's what you tell us!"

"Yes, but –"

"So what can I do about your decision? How do I get you to change it?"

He looked at me in a funny way. "You don't. You – stay still, Bernie. If you wiggle, I'll poke you with a safety pin and you'll scream and then how will I feel?"

"Come on, Dad. You're always telling us not to give up. You're always telling us not to take no for an answer."

"I am?"

"How, if we try hard enough, we can do anything."

"That sounds more like your mother than me, Jane. Honestly, I believe in taking what fate dishes out. I'm a stoic. A moral pacifist. There, Bernie, you're done."

"I really want those earrings. And I'm going to get them."

"What do you think I look like, Jane?" Bernie asked.

Well, he was a little kid wrapped up in toilet paper. Dark brown hair showed through. I didn't want to tell him what he looked like.

"Very scary," I said.

"I want to see." Bernie ran to the hall, trailing paper behind him. He's not tall enough to see himself in the hall mirror, so he pulled a stool over and climbed up.

"Honestly, Dad. I am going to keep talking until you do something. Until you go to the earring store and tell the lady what you think."

"I want you to be happy, Janey. You know that. But –"

"One quick visit. Don't do it for yourself. Do it for me."

He smiled down at me. "Tell you what – I'll call and make an appointment sometime. How's that?"

"I've already made the appointment," I said. "Adrienne is expecting us at her store at 7:30 tonight."

"Tonight? What if your mom is late?"

"She won't be late. I called her office to confirm her schedule."

He opened his mouth, then closed it. He sighed, but with a smile on his face. "A chip off the old block," he said. "Jane, you are going to make someone a wonderful boss."

I didn't say anything.

"Okay," he said.

When Bernie saw himself in the mirror, he screamed.

"A mummy!" he shouted. "Help, Daddy, there's a mummy!"

That sounded kind of funny to me too.

"Nobody move!" I call out.

I walk across the floor to the coach. Mr. Gebohm. What a turnip-head. No, that's an insult to turnips. What a Gebohm. "Excuse me," I say, loud as I can. He doesn't even look over at me. "Excuse me! This is our practice time."

He can hear me. He looks down at me and then away. He blows his whistle, and the drill changes. Now the boys are feeding each other passes as they run toward the net for layups.

I march right up to him. I stand as tall as I can. I am not going to be shorter than I have to be. I still don't know how I'm going to get my way, but I know that I have to start by getting him to admit that I am here.

"Hey, Mr. Gebohm!" I say. Over and over. I'm right beside him. I'm right next to him. I'm on his heels, yakking into his ear. He can hear me all right. "Hey, Mr. Gebohm! Hey, Mr. Gebohm! Hey, Mr. Gebohm!" He moves down the sideline. I follow him. He moves onto the court. I'm right there in his ear. "Mr. Gebohm! Mr. Gebohm! Mr. Gebohm!!" I'm like the water torture. After a minute or two of this, he can't stand me. He simply can't stand me.

"You!!" he says. Well, who did he think it was? "Peeler! What Is It?" he asks. The boys are in the middle of a passing drill. He turns to glare down at me. "What Is It? What Is It?" A vein is bulging high up on his forehead.

I smile brightly up at him. "This is *our* rehearsal period in the gym," I say. "We've been waiting all week for it. The principal said we could have it."

He ignores me.

"We're putting on *The Nutcracker* at the winter concert on Tuesday. You know, the story with the toy soldiers and the Mouse King and the Candy Princess. It's usually a ballet, but we're doing it more like modern dance. You'll have to send the boys home."

"Go Away!" he roars. Like I'm a dog. "Go On, Get!" He curses for a while. I've heard all the words before, from Grandma.

"No," I say. I look back across the gym. My cast huddle in front of the stage, looking lost and unhopeful.

Mr. Gebohm gestures to the tall captain. "Gill," he says.

I guess Gill is the boy's name. I hope it's short for Gilbert. What kind of parent names their kid after a part of a fish?

"Keep this nuisance away from me, Gill."

I open my mouth. Nuisance? Gill is smiling. He looms over me like a cliff. I come up to his belly button. He smiles down at the top of my head. I stare up at his armpit – not pretty. I look away.

Gill stands between me and the coach. I step to my left, and he steps to his right. He's still in front of me. I'll get through him the way I'll get through *War and Peace*.

The guys are throwing hard passes around. The basketballs fly through the air. I walk away from Gill, and Mr. Gebohm. I look back.

They're smiling at each other. A mistake they regret almost immediately. I march over to the light switches beside the hall doors and push them all down at once.

14

Dead Dead Dead Dead Dead Dead Dead

Darkness. And, for just a moment, silence. I raise my voice. "Cast of *The Nutcracker* – onstage now!"

Then there's a couple of *thwacking* sounds, and cries of pain. The basketballs, which were in midair when the lights went out, have landed.

I hear some scrambling around in front of me. I hear some familiar voices – Justin's stands out – saying, "Come on. Let's go."

Good for him.

I stumble forward. I can make out the shape of the stage ahead of me. I can hear cries of pain from behind me. Also cries of rage, mixed in with some cursing. More Grandma language.

The stage lights are on a grid hanging from the ceiling. The switches working the stage lights are on the wall to the left of the stage – that's the right side as you face it from the audience. I'll be standing there during the performance. There's a phone on the wall, and a place to put my notebook. I hit the switches marked SR and SL – stage right and stage left. The stage lights come up. All of them: reds and blues and greens and whites and yellows. I don't bother adjusting them for atmosphere now.

"On your marks, people," I call loudly. Those crosses I taped down are where they're going to start from.

There is one more switch on the wall, marked HOUSE.

The cast is trying to work out which marks are theirs. Mom and I went to the theater downtown a few weeks ago to see *A Funny Thing Happened on the Way to the Forum*, and I noticed that many of the cast were staring down at the floor during one of the dance numbers. Looking for their marks. *Tsk tsk.* Mom and I shook our heads at each other.

The gym is lit again. Coach Gebohm has found the light switches. "You!" His voice echoes.

I ignore him.

He runs right up to the edge of the stage, where I'm standing. "You – Peeler!" He doesn't climb up. He stands there on the floor of the gym, puffing and panting and throwing his hands around. "You Come Down Off That Stage Or I'm Going To –"

And then he stops. He can't think what he's going to. His face is working like a kicked ants' nest. He's got a round red mark on his cheek – a missed basketball pass.

Gill runs up beside him. "What're we supposed to do next, coach?" he asks.

"Keep practicing! What else? Are we going to let a bunch of . . . of *actors* stop us?" He stares up at me. Of course I'm not an actor. He turns and shouts to his team, "Layup Drill – Starting . . . Now!"

The players start bouncing balls and running to the baskets. Coach Gebohm moves back down the gym. I wait a beat or two, then walk over and hit the light switch marked HOUSE. The gym lights go out.

The bouncing stops. The layups stop, except for one poor guy. He's high in the air when the lights go out, hands over his head, getting ready to dunk the ball. I hear a scream from his direction. I can't see what happens to him. The only lights that are on are the stage lights.

"Cast," I say quietly. "Let's walk through the dance number. I'll count you in."

The gym lights go on again. Coach Gebohm is standing by the wall switch. One of the boys is on the ground. Not the dunker – some other guy. His friends help him up.

I turn the lights off. I hear a snicker from the stage – Michael, I bet. Coach Gebohm turns the gym lights back on.

I turn the lights off – he turns them on. I turn them off – he turns them on. This is a "Bugs Bunny" skit. I feel like I should say *click!* and then he'll turn the lights off for me.

★

"Move a little to the left, Jiri," I say. "Face front. Let us see you." The cast is moving slowly through the dance number. Essa steps out of the line.

"Jane," she says. "I don't think we all got the step-ball-change." Meaning that she and Justin got it, but no one else. A step-ball-change is a dance step where you bounce quickly from foot to foot and back: left-right-left, or right-left-right.

"Start again," I call. "I know it's hard without music."

I turn off the houselights again. Gebohm turns them on. I turn them off. I smile. I actually do. The poor coach doesn't know what he's up against. Doesn't he realize, I'm not going to lose the gym. And I have more power than he does. I can turn off his lights, and he can't turn off mine.

In the glow cast by our stage lights, I can see a couple of the ball players. They're not practicing. They move slowly away from us, toward the center of the gym. One of them is hobbling. Other players are standing around in the flickering light and dark.

Gebohm turns on the lights. I turn them off. On – off. On – off. Strobe effect.

The locker room door squeaks a couple of times. The gym lights go on and off . . . and on and off . . . a little slower now. Maybe Gebohm's fingers are getting tired. Mine aren't. I could do this for hours. The locker room door squeaks again. Fewer and fewer players in the gym.

The dance ends, with everyone except Jiri on their marks.

"Where are you supposed to be?" I ask Jiri.

The gym lights go on. I shut them off.

"I think . . . over by Michael," he says.

"Good for you. That's right. So why are you over there by Justin?"

Jiri smiles. "Because I forgot."

I smile back. "Right."

The locker room door squeaks again. And again. The gym lights stay off. All the ball players have left the gym – it's ours.

I turn on the houselights myself, and step out onto the stage. "Now," I begin, but before I can say another word, the applause starts. I don't know who starts it, but suddenly everyone onstage is clapping. Michael whistles through his teeth. I blush.

I can't talk. I stare at Patti. She's clapping too. Does she still like me? I can't say. I'll never forget what she said to Brad, but I can't help remembering other times we've had together: happy times, laughing times.

Friendship isn't always straight ahead.

I wave my hands to stop the applause. I feel silly. "Thanks," I say. I can't think of anything else. "Thanks."

The gym door opens and Miss Gonsalves comes in with a smile the size of a banana. "Sorry I'm late," she says. "I was talking to the principal." She kicks a basketball out of her way, notices the other balls lying around. "What are these doing here?"

"Um, there was a little problem with Mr. Gebohm," I say. "He wanted to use the gym for basketball practice."

"Oh, dear!" says Miss Gonsalves. "He's such a strange man. I'm glad you were able to deal with him, Jane."

The class look at each other. Michael hoots with laughter. "Oh, yeah, Jane dealt with him all right."

An hour later we've run through the big scene a few more times. The Nutcracker comes to life to defend Maria from Dame Mouserink. In killing her, his sword breaks. The music turns threatening (*dum de dum dum*) and the Mouse King appears in all his seven-headed glory. The mice attack again. (The step-ball-change comes in this bit. It's easier with the music.) Things are looking grim for the toys, and then the Nutcracker borrows a sword from one of the toy soldiers, and attacks the Mouse King. They fight, and the Nutcracker wins. The mice run away.

I'm pleased with the way the scenes look. We'll know more when we get the costumes, but most people can find their marks, so that they end up in the right place after the big dance-fight sequence. Now we're working toward the finale. Maria clasps her hands together and says:

"O Nutcracker, you've saved the day,
Killed the Mouse King: hip hip hurray!
See here, you've chopped off every head –
He's dead dead dead dead dead dead dead!"

I'm pretty proud of these lines – except for the last one, maybe, but if you count you'll notice that there are seven *deads* to stand for the seven heads of the Mouse King. Patti doesn't do much with them. *Dead dead dead* sounds like a kid shooting a pretend machine gun.

The toys are cheering. Brad stands there with his sword in his hands, looking modest, and says:

"Your words are far too kind, Maria,
I only killed the king to free ya.
And now that I'm a prince again,
I'd like to have you share my reign."

Michael doesn't snicker this time, the way he usually does. I stare at Patti as Brad is saying this. His expression is properly wooden. But the look on her face is really swoony. She's slow on her cue.

"Share your reign? Could you explain?" she says. Finally. She's supposed to turn to the audience, but she keeps staring at Brad.

I bite my tongue to stop myself from yelling at her. "Good," I say. "Now, Brad."

He gestures broadly, and takes her hand to lead her away:

"You'll become Princess Maria.
Your subjects all will want to see ya.
(Except for those who'd rather be ya.)"

That's a joke line, of course, and Brad has a smile on his face as he says it. A stiff wooden version of his you-are-special smile.

Jiri moves into position to deliver his line. He checks with me. I nod and give him the thumbs-up. He smiles, spreads his arms in welcome, and –

"Stop! Stop!" Patti steps to the edge of the stage and frowns down at me and Miss Gonsalves. "I don't know why we need to make fun at the end," she says. "This is a happy story. Why can't, um, Brad and I . . ." she blushes ". . . walk into Candyland arm in arm? The other toys can stand in two lines, and we'll walk between them."

"Like at a wedding?" I say.

Now Michael snickers.

Patti is blushing. "Well, yes," she says.

Miss Gonsalves nods her head, considering. "A wedding. Yes, that might work. A more traditional ending to the story. What do you think, Jane?"

I don't know what to say. Part of me wants to wipe the simper off Patti's face. Quite a big part of me, actually. She's got hold of Brad's hand. Before I can say anything, he twists his hand free. It's his left hand. He stares at it – at the wrist, really. That's where his watch is.

"5:00! I'm late! My mom will kill me." He jumps right off the stage and keeps going. Jiri drops his arms, and stares after Brad.

Patti calls, "Wait! Braddie!" but he doesn't even turn around. She clenches her fists.

"He left you at the altar, hey, Patti?" calls Michael. He laughs. I can't help laughing too. Miss Gonsalves smiles.

I think about continuing the rehearsal. We could do the earlier scenes again – the ones without Brad. Miss Gonsalves sees me hesitate. She knows it's late.

"What do you think we should do, Jane?" she asks.

"I want to go home," says Essa.

"I'm hungry," says Michael.

The cast is crowding around the front of the stage, murmuring agreement. They're tired. They've worked hard.

"I'd like to send everyone home," I say, "but I'm afraid of Mr. Gebohm. What if he insists on using the gym on Monday? This might be our last chance to rehearse onstage."

Miss Gonsalves laughs out loud. "He won't be able to insist. Not after my meeting with Mr. Gordon. Do you all know where I was yesterday, when I wasn't in school?"

Headshakes.

"I was visiting a friend at CITY TV. I told him all about our show – how Jane here wrote it, and it's really a student production – and he was really interested. And this afternoon his producer called me about filming us for the news."

Cheers. Except for me. I can't breathe. Justin smooths his shirt automatically. "Let's keep rehearsing," says Patti. "If this is our last chance."

"But it isn't our last chance, Patti," says Miss Gonsalves. "I went to the principal's office after school. When Mr. Gordon heard that we'd be on TV, he was as excited as you are. He guaranteed us the gym Monday after school, for as long as we want it."

More cheers. "So we can go home?" asks Essa.

"What do you say, Jane?"

I swallow. "Home," I say. "Let's go home."

They jump down from the stage and begin collecting their coats and knapsacks. They're all strangely silent. If they're like me, they're thinking about being on TV. And worrying a bit.

Jiri starts to laugh. "Left at the altar," he says. "Like a wedding, yes?"

Michael pats him on the back.

15

Favorite Spoon

When I get home from practice, it's almost dinnertime. Four bells in the middle dogwatch, or something. I can't remember all this sailor stuff. Grandma's in the kitchen. She's got the radio tuned to an incredibly oldies station, and is crooning along with it. Something about doing things her way. She sings, then coughs and spits. I run up to the third floor to see how Dad's doing. Mom's there, peering at a thermometer.

"How is he?" I ask.

She shakes her head, then the thermometer. "He's hot. The doctor said that the fever would probably break tonight or tomorrow. I hope it's soon."

Dad is tossing and turning. His forehead is red and dry. Mom sits down on the office chair and closes her eyes.

"Guess what!" I say. "Our *Nutcracker* is going to be on TV."

"That's wonderful, dear."

"At least, it might be."

"When?"

"Um . . . I don't know."

"Oh." Her eyes are still closed. "Well, it's wonderful news."

The kitchen table is set for four. Bill and Bernie are sitting in their chairs. Grandma is spooning out applesauce for Bernie. With –

"Hey!" say Bill and I at the same time. "That's my spoon."

"Mine!" I say.

"Mine," says Bill.

Grandma gives the spoon to Bernie. He smiles. "Mine, now," he says.

Grandma snorts – that's her kind of humor – and goes back to the stove. Something horrible is steaming away there. She lifts the lid off a big pot and stirs. Bernie takes a mouthful of applesauce with my favorite spoon.

We've always had the spoon. I can remember the feel of it in my mouth when I was even younger than Bernie. Beautifully rounded, with a deep bowl, and soft on the teeth and gums for all it's made of metal. A perfect spoon for picking up the last bits of cereal from the bottom of the bowl, or for stirring hot chocolate so that the cocoa bits melt into the water or milk, or for holding a too-hot mouthful steady, so that you can cool it without spattering yourself or the table.

Bernie holds the empty spoon out in front of Bill, then jerks it away. Then holds it out again. Bill takes it.

"Hey!" says Bernie.

"Grandma, I want the spoon," says Bill. "I always pick it out of the drawer."

"Why should you get it, Bill?" I ask. "You had it at dinner last night."

"Well, you used it for breakfast this morning."

"Did not. I gave it to Bernie."

We both stare at Bernie. He opens his mouth, then closes it. Looks away. He knows that he shouldn't get the spoon for two meals in one day. I reach across to grab it. Bill sticks out his elbow, catching me under the chin. It hurts. I punch him back. (Not *back*, because he didn't really punch me first.)

"Grandma, Jane hurt me." The big baby.

"You hurt me first. And anyway, you asked for it."

"Did not."

"I'm hungry," says Bernie. "And I don't have a spoon."

Bill tries to flip the spoon and catch it – and, of course, it goes flying. Bill pretended to be a magician once. He went around in a cape and top hat, saying "hey presto pass" and "abracadabra" and trying to pull trick flowers out of things. One of his short-lived fads. He's not very well coordinated. Neither am I. None of us is. Dad trying to catch a football is one of the funniest things I have ever seen.

The spoon clatters across the floor, ending up by the stove. Before any of us can move, Grandma's foot flashes out. She steps on the spoon, then, slowly, bends down and picks it up. She holds the spoon where we can all see it, and opens the cupboard under the sink – that's where we keep our kitchen garbage. Our jaws drop. Her face is as still as stone. She drops the spoon into the garbage, and closes the cupboard door.

The potatoes are a bit pasty, and the brussels sprouts – they were in the big smelly pot – well, they're brussels sprouts. Not my favorite food. And the ham is dry. But nothing is horrible. For one of Grandma's meals, it's a triumph.

I'm surprised Bill isn't eating much. He likes plain meat and potatoes.

Grandma doesn't ask us how our day went. I tell her anyway. "Guess what?" I say. "The basketball coach was being really mean today." I tell her about the fight with Mr. Gebohm.

She snorts. "He sounds like a real dastard."

"Better be careful of old Gebohm," says Bill. "He's mean. David laughed at him when he was showing us how to do a layup, and missed. Gebohm turned all red, and started shouting."

"Yes, he did that this afternoon," I say.

"And then he made David do push-ups for the rest of the period. Whenever he sees David now, he makes him do more push-ups."

"Are you going to eat your ham, William?" asks Grandma.

"I'm not really hungry," he says.

She reaches over with her fork, spears his meat, and puts it on her own plate. "Well, I'll take it," she says. She doesn't seem too upset.

Dessert is burnt pudding – doesn't taste very good. Bill finishes his. So does Bernie. I eat a few bites. It would probably taste better with my favorite spoon.

After dinner I go to my room, and start on my homework. I see a note to myself from last week. 1950s ARTIFACT.

Drat.

I haven't thought about it at all. *Just a little something. A diary, maybe; or a souvenir from that time. A piece of history,* Miss Gonsalves said.

"Dad?" I call out. "Do you –" then I realize he's not here. Maybe Mom can help.

I go downstairs and find her and Grandma in the family room.

"Mom, do you have any artifacts from the 1950s?" I ask.

"What?"

I repeat my question. Mom frowns. She's thinking of something else.

Bill comes in from the kitchen. He does his homework there. "David has a gun from the 1950s. A pistol. It's in a case. He showed it to me."

"A pistol? How come he has a pistol?"

"It was his grandfather's. David's grandfather was in the Israel Defence Force in 1956. He fought in the Sinai campaign. He met Moshe Dayan."

Can I hand in David's grandfather's pistol as my artifact? I don't think so.

"David is named after him," Bill goes on.

"After Moshe Dayan?"

"No, his grandfather."

"His grandfather is named after Moshe Dayan?" I'm just kidding; I know what Bill means. And he knows I know.

"Shut up," he says.

"You shut up."

"No, you."

"I knew a man named Moshe once," says Grandma. She looks a long way back. Some of the wrinkles in her forehead smooth out. "Before I met your father," she adds to Mom.

"I'm going to check on Alex," Mom says.

"You want me to get you some dinner?" Grandma asks.

"No. I'm, uh, not hungry." Running past me and up the stairs, Mom looks very young, a little girl caught in a white lie.

16

Where There's Smoke . . .

I sleep badly. In my dream I'm wading through mud. Thick mud that clings to my dress, to my hands. I'm running away. The seven-headed Mouse King is after me. Every one of his heads looks like Mr. Gebohm. I trip and fall, making a big crash. King Gebohm comes closer. He's holding a scepter in one paw. I start doing push-ups in the mud. He hits me with his scepter. I don't feel anything, but I hear the *thump* of the scepter hitting me. I cry for help. Usually when you cry for help in your dream, nothing comes out. Nothing comes out this time, either. Then Mr. Gebohm opens his mouth, and lets loose a high-pitched squeak. It echoes across the muddy field in my dream. He hits me again and again. *Thump. Thump. Thump.*

I wake up. The thumping is real. It's coming from downstairs. Is the squeaking real, too? I can hear Grandma, but she's not squeaking. She's swearing.

"Come back, you little dastard!"

And another *thump*.

I put on my slippers and go to the hallway. There's a crash, and some more swearing from Grandma. I run downstairs. The lights are on. Grandma's in the hallway with a broom in her hands, a cigarette in the corner of her mouth, and a wild look in her eyes.

"I've chased him all around the downstairs," she says, panting.

"Who?"

She points down at the floor. "There! See him?" She swings the broom in a vicious arc.

Thump.

So that's the noise I heard.

"Missed! Son of a. . . ." Grandma runs down the hall toward the kitchen. I follow to the doorway, and stop there to stare.

The kitchen is a mess. The cupboards under the sink and counter, where we keep the pots and pans, have their doors open. The garbage can under the sink is on its side, and there's garbage everywhere. The toaster has fallen off the counter. (Was that the crash I heard in my dream?) It's on the floor, its cord stretched taut back to the wall.

"Got him now!" says Grandma. "He's trapped, the little devil." She stands near the toaster, with her broom raised in both hands. I walk closer, and hear, very faintly, a high-pitched squeaking.

I begin to have a suspicion.

"What seems to be the trouble?" asks a weak but familiar voice from behind me.

I turn around. "Daddy!"

He smiles at me, but it looks wrong somehow. Empty. It's his smile, but there's no him behind it. A scary sight. Even scarier than Grandma swinging a broom in the middle of the night.

"Alexander!" Mom is right behind him. "Get back to bed. You're sick. And what are you all doing up, children? You go to bed too." I didn't hear my brothers come downstairs but there they are in the doorway, hopping up and down, trying to see.

Mom doesn't tell Grandma to go to bed. "What are you doing, Mother?" she asks.

Grandma turns the toaster right side up. It's still plugged into the wall above the countertop. The broom is poised in her hand.

"He was hiding in there. Now I've chased him back."

"Who was hiding, Mother?"

"He thinks he's safe, but I'm going to smoke him out."

Grandma pushes down the knob that starts the toaster.

I don't *know* what is going on. I really don't. And yet, maybe because of the dream, maybe because of what is going on at school, I suspect. . . . No. It can't be. And yet there's Grandma, poised, ready to pounce. She looks like a tough old tabby waiting in front of a . . .

Could it be?

We wait. The coils inside the toaster glow. Grandma smiles.

"I think," says Dad, "that I – oh, *no!*"

He jumps. I jump too. We all jump. None of us as high as the mouse trapped inside the toaster. He – or she, I never do find out – jumps three or four times its own height. Its entire body is visible in the air, well above the clear of the dented chrome crumb-strewn top. Its tail flails back and forth.

Dad darts forward. Grandma swings her broom like a baseball bat. She'd hit a home run with the mouse, only Dad gets in the way. The broom hits him in the leg. *Thump.* He winces. She draws back and swings again, but she's too late. With a clearly audible squeak, the mouse scampers under the refrigerator.

She swears. "After all this chasing. You know, I found the ham thing inside the toaster. Two inches away from my face."

So my suspicions are right. There really is a mouse in the house. I must have known all along. That's why my dreams were all confused, with the Mouse King and the squeaking. That's the reason for the bowling. I shudder, thinking how close I was, that time in the basement in the dark. Mice.

I wonder what Grandma was doing, two inches away from the toaster late at night.

"Was that a mouse?" asks Mom. "A mouse in our house?" She sounds like she's reading a cute little picture book.

"It's gone to the basement," says Bernie. He's standing at the top of the stairs.

"Good," says Grandma. "That's where I set the traps."

"Traps?" Bill turns on the basement light. "Can I see?"

"Mousetraps? There's mousetraps in our house?" Mom's cute little picture book takes a surprising turn. Not too often that you get a cute little picture of a mutilated mouse. "Where'd the mousetraps come from?"

"Grandma," I say. "Grandma, *you* did it. That's why you wanted to know where the hardware store was."

"But why didn't you tell me, Mother?"

Grandma doesn't reply. If anything, she looks embarrassed.

"Because she didn't want to worry you," I say.

Dad isn't paying any attention. He's on his hands and knees, picking up apple cores and uneaten bits of sandwich and throwing them back into the garbage container. "Oh dear, oh dear," he says. "Look at all this mess."

A mouse in the toaster. I swallow unhappily, thinking back to the toast I've eaten over the past week. Mouse toast. Yuck. I think about sailor Bill, and all his hard tack.

"*Hey!*" says Bernie.

"Go to bed, Bernie," says Mom. "You too, Jane and Bill."

"I'm not going to bed before Bill," I say.

"*Hey!*" says Bernie again. He points at the toaster. "It's on –"

"*Fire!*" says Bill.

If you're trying to get someone's attention, it's much better to say "fire" than "hey." Everyone shuts up and stares.

The toaster is smoking even more than usual. And a small tongue of fire pokes itself out of the slot the way you might poke your tongue out to lick around the edge of your mouth.

Grandma acts first. She drops the broom and reaches over to unplug the toaster. "Do you have an extinguisher?" she asks Mom.

We do. Before Mom can answer, I scramble onto the counter and open the utility cupboard. We keep all the dangerous stuff up here, out of Bernie's reach. Drain cleaner and floor cleaner and turpentine in case he swallows them and poisons himself. Plastic bags in case he puts them over his head and suffocates. Picture wire in case he – I don't know what – strangles himself, maybe. Cough syrup. Pills. More plastic bags. More medicine. Somewhere at the back is a portable fire extinguisher.

"Be careful, Jane!" calls Mom.

Dad is washing his hands in the sink – his hands and what he's holding in them. "Who threw this out?" he asks, drying it carefully on a tea towel. "This is my favorite spoon."

The fire seems to be dying on its own, but there's still lots of smoke. I find the extinguisher. Mom leads Dad out of the kitchen, calling over her shoulder for us to come too. "In a minute," I say. I can't get the extinguisher to work. Neither can Grandma.

Bill jumps from foot to foot. Grandma squeezes the extinguisher trigger again; and again; nothing. There's less and less smoke.

"Let me try," says Bill.

"And me!" says Bernie. "I want a turn."

"No, let me," says Bill. "Before it's too late."

"This isn't a ham game," says Grandma.

The fire burns out. There doesn't seem to be any smoke at all. Bill sighs.

Grandma lifts the toaster off the floor, turns it over, and shakes it into the sink. No mouse inside, thank goodness. Nothing inside but toast crumbs. Quite a lot of crumbs, actually.

"Just as well we didn't use the extinguisher," she says. "That chemical foam is just shell to get off. Now the toaster's as good as new."

"How did you know we had a mouse, Grandma?" I ask. Bill and Bernie are in the basement, checking the traps.

"Mice," says Grandma. "No one has one mouse, unless it's a pet." Grandma plugs in the toaster, and turns it on.

"Mice, then. How did you know we had mice?"

"I heard them, the first night I was here, rolling up and down the walls."

Rolling? "Like marbles?" I say. "Mice make a sound like marbles? Or bowling balls?"

Grandma nods. Bill and Bernie come upstairs. They're disappointed. I can tell without having to hear them say it that the traps are empty.

I don't know how I feel about that. I don't want mice in the house, but I don't want them caught in the traps, either. In my heart I like the cute little picture book mice – as long as they stay in the books.

"What did you use for bait?" asks Bill. "I didn't see any cheese."

"Cheese gets stale. Better to use peanut butter."

"Mice eat peanut butter?" asks Bernie, yawning hugely. "Like me?"

The toaster is working. The heating coils are glowing red. Grandma bends down to light her cigarette off one. "Little dastards'll eat anything." She notices me staring at her. So that's what she was doing, inches away from the toaster.

"Out of matches," she says.

★

135

"Mother! Mother, look at this!" Mom runs into the kitchen, holding the thermometer. Her face is shining. She's so beautiful. "Alex is sweating!"

"So what? I'm sweating myself. All that running around."

"Don't you see? It means the fever's broken. He's asleep now, but I took his temperature before he dropped off. It's lower than it was. See?"

She notices us then. "Why aren't you children in bed?"

"Is Daddy getting better?" I ask.

"Yes." She relaxes, smiles at me. "Yes, he is."

"Good."

"Yes. Now go to bed."

She kisses us all good night and walks us upstairs. I fall asleep right away. I don't dream at all. Not about fire, or bowling, or anything. When I wake up in the morning, the sun is streaming through my window. My pajamas smell of burnt toast.

17

O Christmas Tree

"Here's the one," says Grandma. Our corner fruit store sells Christmas trees around the back. Every year Dad takes us to pick one out. Not this year, of course. Dad had breakfast this morning, for the first time in a while, but he's not going outside yet. He's upstairs sleeping now, and Grandma is taking us tree shopping. A typical winter weekend in Toronto, warm enough to melt the snow, but freeze you. Copernicus, the big market street, is crowded with people. Parkas are open at the throat, breath steams, slush collects at the side of the roads.

Grandma's choice is a scrawny spruce. It's lying down on the ground. It looks tired.

"That's the tree. Let's go home."

We all stare at her.

"It's not the biggest!" says Bernie. "That one is bigger!" He stands up in his stroller to point to one of the standing trees. A pine. I like pine myself. The long needles make it look fuller.

"Or how about this one?" I say. "See Grandma, it's bushier than yours."

"So what? This is the one. Let's go. You wanted me to take you to look for a Christmas tree, and I found you one."

"But –"

"Nope." She picks up the tree. It's not very big at all. Grandma is an old lady, and she can lift it with one hand.

"Are we done already, Jane?" asks Bernie, twisting in his stroller.

"I guess so," I say.

"But I like to pick," says Bernie.

Dad's Christmas tree shopping expeditions always take a long time. We check out every tree. There's a lot of comparing and arguing; we usually end up standing the trees next to each other to see which one is the tallest. Sometimes we have to toss a coin. Then, when we've made our choice, we have to get the tree home. If there's snow, we drag it home on a toboggan. If there isn't enough snow for a toboggan, we put the tree on Bernie's stroller. Bill and I push. Dad and Bernie steer. By the time we get home with the tree, we feel that we've earned our hot chocolate.

"So what?" says Grandma. She walks away. We hurry after her. I'm pushing Bernie in his stroller. When Grandma gets to the slushy sidewalk, I grab her arm.

"You have to pay Tom," I say. Tom runs the fruit store. He's not giving the trees away.

"I paid him before we went out back," she says. "Come on, now." She carries the tree to the corner.

"The tree should be bigger," I say. "And bushier. Shouldn't it, Bill?"

He shrugs. "I guess so," he says.

What's wrong with Bill? He's usually as keen as the rest of us.

"It's only a tree," he says.

"A Christmas tree," I remind him. "A tree with presents under it."

"You don't need a tree to get presents," he says. "David gets presents without a tree."

"David's Jewish," I say. "He doesn't get presents without a whatchamacallit candleholder."

"Menorah." He smiles at me condescendingly. I hate it when he knows something I don't. He sounds the word out slowly, like I'm an idiot. "And it's not for presents. It's just a symbol of the miracle."

"Yeah, well, so's a Christmas tree a symbol. Isn't it?" I ask Grandma.

"Christmas tree? It's a nuisance," says Grandma. "It falls over. It dries out. It's messy. The needles get everywhere. I can't stand the ham things."

"The tree should be in my stroller. That's how Daddy does it," says Bernie. "You're not doing it right, Grandma."

"Uh-huh," says Grandma. She drags the tree down the street to the corner with a crosswalk. We follow. She sticks out her pointing finger. A car moving up the street doesn't stop at the crosswalk; doesn't even slow down. Neither does the car after it.

"Dastards!" She changes fingers.

The next car is slowing down. So is the one coming from the opposite direction.

"Come on!" Grandma looks back at us, and strides out into the crosswalk.

We hang back. "Watch out, Grandma!" I call.

Copernicus Street is famous for its double U-turns. That's where a car going up the street makes a U-turn at the same time as a car going down the street. They slow down, then crisscross around each other in the middle of the intersection. It's a kind of traffic ballet – a stately circle dance.

That's what's going on now. Only now there's another ballerina onstage. Grandma. And she doesn't know the dance.

"What the shell is going on?" She glares at the nearest driver. He has one of those ugly old cars, big as a boat. His window is rolled down, so he can call out to someone he knows on the street.

"Hey, axle!" That's what it sounds like Grandma calls him. "Watch where you're going!"

The driver stares at her. He has a cigar in his mouth, and it hangs out at a ludicrous angle. His car keeps coming. It's getting close to Grandma.

She hoists the tree onto her shoulder. Good thing it's a small tree. It's between her and the big old ugly car. The car keeps coming. Closer and closer. Is it going to run her over? I'd be trying to get out of the way, but Grandma doesn't. She stands her ground. When the car is close enough, she lunges forward and sticks the scrawny Christmas tree right in the open window. She uses both hands to ram the tree right into the car, point first.

The car swerves the wrong way, toward the oncoming traffic, which stops. The car keeps going, slowly, until it crashes into a streetlight. And stops. The Christmas tree is still sticking out of the driver's window, bouncing from the impact.

Grandma walks back to where we're waiting on the sidewalk. Her face is expressionless.

The driver opens his door and crawls out. His face is covered in pine needles. His cigar is still in his mouth. He's upset. He yanks the tree out of his window and throws it on the ground. There aren't a lot of needles left on the tree now. Most of them are on him.

"Hey!" says Bernie to me. "That's our tree."

"Sh," I say.

"What are we going to do for a Christmas tree now?"

Grandma bends down. "We'll get another one," she says clearly. As she walks us back to the fruit store, people stare at us and whisper and chuckle. One word I recognize: "olé."

That's it! That's what Grandma's gesture reminded me of. A matador, when he's sticking the bull.

The next tree we pick out is bigger than the first one. We load it into Bernie's stroller and walk it across Copernicus very carefully. The big old car is still pointing the wrong way, blocking traffic.

We lean the tree against the side of the front porch, like we always do, and troop in for hot chocolate. There's a surprise waiting for us in the hall. Dad. He says hello to us all, a bit shyly. "I saw you carrying the tree up the steps. Nice looking one this year. Did you have fun picking it out? Have you earned your hot chocolate?"

Funny to hear him say that – usually it's Mom.

"Oh, yes," says Bill. "Especially Grandma."

"Got anything stronger than hot chocolate?" asks Grandma.

Dad starts to laugh, and then it turns into a cough, and he has to go to the living room and sit down. I go with him, and sit on the arm of his chair. "So, how are you doing, Daddy? How are you doing really?"

"I'm weak, but I feel a lot better."

He smiles. He looks thinner and tireder than normal, but his eyes are the same as always. It's him again. I lean over and give him a hug. It's nice to have him back.

"I missed you."

His bathrobe rides up his arms. His wrists look small and bony.

"I've missed you too. How's my little girl? How's the show going?"

"It's going well. We might be on TV. I'm a little worried about Jiri, who may not be able to memorize his part, but everyone likes the play, except for Mr. Gebohm, who's trying to kill us."

"Oh, dear."

"Dad, can I ask you a question?"

"Sure, honey." He settles back in the chair.

"I have a friend," I say.

"Is this about your friend, or about you?" asks Dad. "I'm not going to give fatherly advice to your friend. I'm not her father."

"Oh, it's about me. But suppose my friend isn't . . . well, suppose she seems to be not really my friend right now. How do I know if it's forever, or if she'll come back?"

"Go on," says Dad. He clasps his hands together and listens.

I tell my dad about me and Patti. It's been troubling me. I've known Patti since kindergarten, and we've always done things together. It's a great comfort knowing who your best friend is. And now, suddenly, I don't. I don't call her when I get home. I don't tell her the things that are on my mind. I don't even hang out with her at recess. This is the first time I can remember when I didn't know who I'd do my next group project with. It's strange. I'm entering a new country, and I don't know the language.

"It's about trust, really," I say. "I can't trust Patti anymore. And that makes me sad."

Silence from the chair. I look down. Dad is dozing quietly.

Hmm. I guess my problems are not that exciting.

"Hot chocolate in the kitchen," Grandma calls. I give Daddy a kiss on his forehead and get up from the chair. His forehead isn't hot. He sighs and keeps breathing steadily.

Bill and Bernie are fighting over the cup with Captain Hook on it. "Perfect for six-water grog," says Bill. "Splice the main brace."

"I want to splice the main brace too," says Bernie.

"Splice it with the Winnie the Pooh cup," says Bill.

"It's not the same."

I don't care which cup I get. I take a sip – from Bart Simpson – and nearly spit it out. It's lumpy. So's my next sip. And the one after that. And the sips that aren't lumpy are too watery. Grandma has found a way to ruin instant hot chocolate. I didn't think you could do that.

Bernie's kneeling in a regular chair. He leans over the table. "Grandma, do you want to play –"

"In a minute," she says.

Grandma has a glass in her hand. She drinks, sighs.

"What's that?" Bernie asks.

"Single malt hot chocolate," says Grandma.

18

I Shouldn't Be Having This Conversation

Sunday afternoon. Dad is upstairs, resting. His temperature is almost normal now. Mom is at the office, catching up. Grandma has gone back to her apartment to pick up something – she won't say what.

Lunch is over. Bill and Bernie are fighting around the kitchen, using paper towel rolls for swords. Watching them, I can't help thinking about the choreography of the fight scene in our *Nutcracker*.

"Yoicks!" says Bernie, swinging his sword wildly. "Yoicks! Yoicks! Yoicks!"

"Stop shouting, Bernie," I say. "And slow down. They'll never see you if you flail around like that."

"Huh?"

"And Bill, could you come forward a bit. Maybe *three* steps. Left-right-left."

"Huh?"

"It's stronger that way. Try it again, you guys." I sit back.

They look at each other, shrug their shoulders, and go back to their fighting as if I had never opened my mouth. "Yoicks! Yoicks! Yoicks!" says Bernie.

Hard to be the director in your own home. The actors don't have to do what you say. I miss my *Nutcracker*.

As if on cue, the phone rings, and the ident-a-call screen says OGILVY. It's my Nutcracker: Brad. "Hello!" I say.

Only it's not Brad. A strange woman's voice on the other end of the phone says, "Is that Jane? Jane Peeler?"

"Yes. Who's this?"

"I'm Mrs. Ogilvy. Brad Ogilvy's mother. Tell me, dear, how are you?"

"Fine," I say. "Um, how are you?"

"I can't talk for long. Brad doesn't know I'm calling."

I don't say anything.

"It's about the project you and Brad are doing together. I wondered how it's going."

"Huh?"

"We talked about it when I saw you at the hospital a few days ago. A science project, wasn't it?"

"Um."

"You remember, don't you, dear? About . . . nuts?"

"Oh, *that* project."

My brothers are still fighting in the kitchen. Bill slashes with his paper towel roll at Bernie, who ducks and stabs blindly forward, hitting Bill in the nose.

Blood spurts. Bill puts his hands to his nose. They come away bloody. Bill starts to cry. Bernie drops his sword. The look on his face is almost religious – a mixture of fear, awe, and surprised delight.

"Yes, dear. You were working on it after school on Friday, weren't you? You and Brad."

"I was with Brad after school, yes."

"Can you tell me how it's going?"

"Um . . . why can't you ask your son – Brad?" I say.

And now she gets weird. All right, weirder. "Because, you see, dear, I don't trust Brad," she says. "I ask him about it and he says it's going fine. But I don't see any work in his notebook. I go through his school-work when he's asleep, and I can't find anything about nuts."

"Oh." I say. I'm definitely not comfortable with this. I don't think she should be going through Brad's notebook. I don't think he should be lying to his mom. I don't think I should be having this conversation.

"I know about the maps you're all making for geography. I know about the 1950s artifact. Brad is going to bring in a BAN THE BOMB button we found in the basement. But I can't find anything about nuts. So, what's going on?" Mrs. Ogilvy asks. Her voice is getting harsher. "What's he up to? What secret is he keeping from his mother?"

"I don't know," I say.

Bill is sniffing. His shirt is sprinkled with bloody drops. Bernie reaches up to touch one.

"Aha!" Mrs. Ogilvy's voice rings down the phone like a trumpet. "So there *is* a secret!"

"Huh? I mean, there is?"

"You just admitted it."

"I did?"

"What is it? What is Brad's secret? Tell me. I have a right to know. Tell me what he's hiding from his mother!"

"I think I have to go," I say. "My brother is bleeding."

"What? What was that?"

"Bill's hurt," I say.

She doesn't hear me. "Filbert?" she says. "What about filberts? Is that what the nut project is about?"

I hang up.

Bill and Bernie both have blood on their hands. I don't want to wake up Dad. I'm supposed to be responsible. "Are you okay, Bill?" I ask.

"No."

"How about you, Bernie?"

"Yoicks!" says Bernie.

19

Both My Parents

Both my parents are up early Monday morning. Both my parents are in the kitchen. Maybe this happens to you all the time, but for me it's a real treat.

"I'm fine, dear," says Dad. I wonder if he is fine. His voice is stronger, but he looks a bit shaky. "Eat up, Bernie. Breakfast doesn't get better than this."

Bernie looks up from his cereal. It's chilly in our kitchen, and he's shivering in his pajamas. "It doesn't?"

Mom is putting on her overcoat. She peers at Dad, with her head on one side. "I don't know, Alex. I'm worried about you. The doctor said to be careful you don't try to do too much too quickly."

"Doctors! What do they know?" says Dad heartily. "Hey there, Jane. Can I pour you some cereal?"

"I can get my own," I say. "I don't want you –"

"Nonsense. I'm in great shape. A bit of a cough is all I have."

He does have it, too. He coughs as he's pouring my cereal, so that some of it spills.

"No problem." Dad sweeps up the cereal into his hand, and dumps it in the garbage.

"So is Grandma leaving now?" asks Bernie.

Both parents answer together.

"Of course," says Dad.

"No," says Mom.

Bernie looks at me. I shrug.

"Well, that settles it," says Dad.

"Alex, you're in no position to look after things here."

"Yes, I am," says Dad.

"You are not."

"I am, I tell you."

"Are not."

Dad looks at me. "You're supposed to say 'am so,'" I tell him.

"Thanks." He sticks out his tongue at me. A very Dad-like gesture. I have to laugh. Maybe he is all right.

"Let *me* see that." Mom turns him around so that he's facing her. "I don't know how healthy that looks."

"Hey, Dad!" It's Bill. "Why are you sticking your tongue out at Mom?"

"She asked me to." Dad stares at him. "You're all dressed. Wow. Do you have socks on both feet?"

"Course. This is my number one shore-going rig."

"It's dress rehearsal day. The winter concert is tomorrow," I say.

Bill moves to stand between me and Dad. "Our class is going to do way better than Jane's class."

"You are not." I try to shift him. We shove each other.

"We are so!"

"Are not!!"

"Are too!!"

Actually, he may have a point. I have this momentary image of Jiri forgetting his big line in front of the parents and kids and CITY TV news cameras and everything. . . .

"You're supposed to say 'are not,'" Dad reminds me in a whisper.

"Thanks," I tell him.

"And don't be so competitive, you two," says Mom. She doesn't like it when we compare.

Not that there's any contest. "I'm way less competitive than Bill is," I say.

"No way!" he says quickly. "I'm less competitive than you are."

"Yo *ho*! You wouldn't know how to spell competitive," I say.

"Yo ho *ho*! You wouldn't know where to *look* for it!" He snaps his fingers in my face. Triumph.

"That," I say quietly, "is because I'm not as competitive as you." I smile.

"I . . . you. . . ." His face turns three shades of red.

Got him.

"Is Grandma staying or not?" Bernie still wants to know.

"No," says Dad. "I'll drive her home this morning." Then he starts to cough. A pretty good one. He holds on to the counter.

"I don't think –" Mom begins.

"Good!" says Bernie. "I'm glad Grandma's going."

"Hurray!" says Bill.

"Oh, come on," Mom sighs. "Try to be nice about Grandma. I asked her to come, and she said yes. She didn't have to."

"But you asked her," says Bernie. "We always have to do what you say."

"But –"

"Even Daddy does what you say."

"The boy has a point there, honey," says Dad. "You have a way of making people do your bidding."

I think back to the gym, yesterday, with Mr. Gebohm. I *knew* I would get my way. Dad says that I remind him of Mom sometimes. Maybe that's what he means. We don't look alike. She's tall and beautiful and has this amazing chestnut colored hair. I'm short for my age, and my hair is plain brown, unless I dye it. And no one has ever called me beautiful.

There's a scratching noise in the hall. A mouse? Doesn't sound quite right. I listen, but I don't hear it again.

Mom is blushing. She makes herself busy, unbuttoning and then rebuttoning her coat. "Anyway, it's not easy for Grandma, being here in a strange place with three – four – people to look after."

"Thank *you*," says Dad.

"She doesn't play with me," says Bernie.

"She hates us," says Bill.

They look at me.

I'm thinking back to last summer, when Grandma and I actually laughed together for a while – a very short while. We were on our way to Aunt Vera's, and Grandma helped me smuggle a homeless guy named Marty into the back of the family van. She said I was full of moxie.

"What about the mousetraps?" I say. "She helped there."

Bill nods, conceding the mousetraps. "Nothing in them this morning," he says. He and Bernie have been checking every few hours since they found out about them.

"What mousetraps?" asks Dad.

"And the Christmas tree," I say. "The first one, at the crosswalk. That was . . ."

"Not uncool," says Bill.

"That big car went right into the pole," says Bernie, with a smile that goes past his cereal spoon.

"What big car?" asks Dad.

"But she's kind of a lousy cook," says Bill. He pulls a loaf out of the bread drawer, and looks around for the big knife.

My turn to nod. No argument there. Saying Grandma is kind of a lousy cook is like saying that the CN Tower is kind of tall, or that the Rolling Stones are kind of old.

"Well, I like her," I say. "For all she's grumpy and hard."

"And she still smokes," says Bernie. "That's bad, isn't it, Mom?"

"Yes, honey."

"And she says words like –"

"Yes," says Mom quickly.

"Let me, Bill," says Dad, taking the knife from Bill's hand.

I hear another sound from the hallway – a match being struck. A moment later I can smell the sulfur from the match head.

"So is Grandma going to stay or go?" Bernie still wants to know.

"Good question," says Grandma herself, appearing in the doorway in her bathrobe, hairnet, and morning cigarette.

"Mother-in-law!" says Dad. "We were just talking about you."

"Yeah?"

Did she hear? Did she hear us say how horrible she was? I blush deeply, thinking she may have heard all that. It's awful to hear bad things about yourself. I know.

Hey. I *do* know.

Grandma is pouring coffee from the pot. Her hair is the color of iron filings behind the hairnet. There are dark stains under her eyes.

"Well, now that I'm here, I guess I better put together those school lunches. I started a mold last night. Unless I'm going home." She puts down her cigarette to take a sip of coffee. "So, am I going home?"

"Well, I got up feeling much better this morning," Dad begins. "But I don't. . . ." He pauses, screws up his face.

Grandma stands quietly, smoking and drinking coffee.

"Maybe it's best if. . . ." And he starts coughing.

Bill is over by the calendar. "Today is the first day of Chanukah," he says.

"*Gut yontiff*," says Grandma, without looking at him.

"Hey, I didn't know you knew any Yiddish."

"A lot you don't know about me, sailor boy."

"I'm late for a meeting," says Mom. "Alex, sit down!"

Dad slides into a chair. His face is the color of the snow outside – that is, whitish gray. Mom hurriedly rebuttons her coat. "Please stay, Mother."

She heads down the hallway without waiting for an answer.

"Now, let's see what you'll be having for lunch." Grandma reaches deep into the refrigerator, and pulls out a bowl of . . . something that wiggles.

"I don't want mold," says Bill.

"Don't be silly. This isn't mold, sailor boy. It's *a* mold. A jelly mold. I made some calves' foot jelly for your father's lunch."

Dad groans. Bill looks relieved and apprehensive at the same time. "What am I getting?"

"Don't worry. There'll be some left over for you too. Won't that be tasty?"

Is there, or is there not, a suspicion of a gleam in Grandma's eye?

Bill groans. The bowl wiggles. Dad goes back upstairs to bed.

20

The Last Cookie

I don't have anyone to tell my mouse-in-the-toaster story to at school. Normally I'd tell Patti, but now I don't want to. I keep hearing her voice telling Brad how bossy I am. Her smile for me today, her concern for my dad, seem false. Maybe they aren't. Maybe she still likes me, sort of. But I don't like her as much as I used to. I tell her my dad is doing fine.

Miss Gonsalves has moved us around. Now I'm sitting beside Zillah. Zillah the dark-haired, dark-eyed, dark-souled girl. She's tall and thin, and wears black clothes and a frown most of the time. Her nose and eyebrow are pierced. I'm afraid of her, a little. There's a power around her, like a dark mist. She was a natural to play the part of Dame Mouserink, the wicked mouse queen in our *Nutcracker*. When I asked her, she didn't thank me or smile or anything, in fact she spat, but after she spat she nodded her head.

We walk out of class together at morning recess, and stay together. Zillah doesn't have many friends. Patti runs off to be near Brad. He's playing basketball with a bunch of other guys and girls. Patti watches.

Mr. Gebohm is on playground duty. I watch him out of the corner of my eye, the way you watch a wasp in the room. He circles away, toward Jiri, who's playing catch with a little kid. Gebohm watches the ball for a moment. When he sees me, he comes over. I shrink inside. Zillah stands impassively. I'm glad she's here.

"Peeler." That's all he says.

"Yes, sir."

He shakes his head. There's a faint red mark on his cheek from Friday night.

"So, Peeler, you are going to take away my gym again."

"Me?" I say.

"Yes. You. You took it away from me once already. Don't You Realize That I Have A Basketball Team To Train? Basketball." He closes his eyes on the word. Holds his hands out in front of him, cupped around a basketball-sized chunk of December air. His intensity is uncomfortable.

"Sorry," I say.

"I tried to tell Mr. Gordon, but he won't listen. Enjoy your rehearsal in my gym this afternoon. And good luck tomorrow night at your *performance*." He laughs – a very sinister laugh – and stalks off.

Oh, no. And I thought our rehearsal problems were over. Now the specter of Mr. Gebohm hangs over the next two days. "What do you think he means?" I ask Zillah. "Is he going to wreck our performance?"

She shrugs.

"What can I do? Should I tell Miss Gonsalves? She'll never believe me. She'll ask what he said, and I'll say he wished me good luck. But I know – I just know – he's going to try to wreck the show."

Zillah shakes her head at me, and sounds those three chords you hear on TV when something bad is about to happen: *dah duh* duhn. I stare at her – this is a joke. The first joke I've ever heard from her. She's not worried about Mr. Gebohm. Not the least bit.

That makes me feel better. I almost laugh. She almost smiles. I'm about to tell her about Grandma and the mouse, only the bell rings to end recess.

Miss Gonsalves makes it official at the start of our dress rehearsal. A videographer from CITY TV will come tomorrow night to film our *Nutcracker* for a spot on the ten o'clock news. There are permission forms for our parents to sign.

We all react in our different ways. I swallow, and feel cold inside, but warm outside. Like a hot butterscotch sundae, I guess. I worry about Mr. Gebohm. Patti is blushing like mad. Michael yowls like a cat.

Justin smooths his hair unnecessarily. Zillah reacts by not reacting. Jiri looks puzzled.

It's 3:30. I start the rehearsal by getting everyone onstage. We'll do five minutes of stretching exercises. Then I've allotted ten minutes to get into costumes, so we'll start promptly at 3:45. "Everyone touch your toes," I yell. "That means you, Michael. Limber up."

"I'm doing my best." He bends a little bit, grimacing mightily.

"Come on! You look as limber as a piece of wood."

"That's not limber. That's lumber. Ha-ha-ha-ha-ha."

The gym door swings open lazily, and Brad enters. I didn't notice he wasn't here.

"Sorry I'm late." He vaults onstage and takes his place between Justin and Patti.

"My, aren't you limber, Braddie!" says Patti.

Rehearsal goes well tonight, until the very end. Almost everyone gets almost all their lines right. Zillah is especially good. A lot of animation – for her. Brad seems a bit low. I try to get him to smile. Michael is an overactor. A ham. But he knows his part so well, I can't really yell at him. And, besides, Patti nudges Brad whenever I open my mouth at all. I feel self-conscious.

And everyone's brought costumes and props from home. Godfather Stahlbaum's gift box in the first scene is huge – a washing machine came in it – and

has a big red bow on top. Justin, playing Fritz, capers
about the stage.

"Godpapa, what *have* you brought us?
What's the present in the box?
Oh, I sure do hope it's not as
Dull as Aunt Irene's dress socks!"

Justin remembers the speech, then loses his con-
centration when he notices a missing button on his
own costume. "Ooh!" he says, his face falling.
Michael laughs and claps him on the back, which is
in character both for him and for the Godfather.
Justin stumbles.

When the Mouse King enters a few scenes later, I
gasp. I've not seen the costume before. It's a giant
construction of cardboard and cloth. Trinley's mom
has done an amazing job. Scary heads glare in all
directions.

Justin screams and jumps away. Very convincing.
The Mouse King lunges after him, then stops.

"Help, I can't see!"

Essa is inside the mouse king costume. She has a
high-pitched mousy voice, which is one of the reasons
I cast her. Also because she's very shy. She's better
inside a costume.

We all laugh. I make a note in my book. I've used
almost all of it now.

★

The last scene starts badly. The Candyland backdrop doesn't fall correctly when Michael pulls the twine holding it up. (I make a note to check it.) Mind you, it looks lovely when we do get it down. Everyone moves slowly and dreamily as the music builds. Patti and Brad walk like a bride and groom through the arch of swords and into the Nutcracker's kingdom, where they are greeted by Jiri, the Herald of Candyland. Jiri moves very gracefully in his costume – a long striped robe that used to be curtains, and a turban made from a big blue towel. He smiles at me because he knows he's at the right place at the right time. He waits for the *dweedle-dweedle*-dee cue, opens his mouth and – nothing comes out.

The music is over now. We're waiting for his lines. But he isn't saying them. Brad and Patti smile at each other. Brad takes her hand and strokes it, playing for time.

I prompt Jiri. "Hail, Prince . . ."

Brad keeps smiling. Patti groans. Jiri's face clears and he starts:

> "Hail, Prince and Princess both,
> From your travels east and, um . . ."

He doesn't finish the line, but goes on to the next one anyway:

> "In Candyland the prospects . . . are nice."

No, they're not. Wrong line. At the piano, Miss Gonsalves is shaking her head.

"Sunshine, and . . . no more mice."

Well, that fits in, but they're not the words I wrote. Jiri can't think of any others.

"I . . . I . . . ding it!"

After the rehearsal I take him aside. He smiles sheepishly down at me.

"I am sorry, Jane. I forgot my lines. I am sorry. I will study. I will."

Miss Gonsalves comes over to put her hand on his arm. She's so comforting. I expect her to offer encouragement, but she surprises me.

"Jiri," she says, "it might be better if you didn't say any lines in the play."

"Huh?"

"You'd still be onstage. In your costume." Her face is full of sympathy. "You just wouldn't say anything."

He turns to me. Miss Gonsalves turns to me too.

"Are the lines too hard, Jiri?" I ask. "Would you like someone else to say them?"

"Oh, no." His big face is horrified. "They are *my* lines. I will learn them."

Patti runs over in her overcoat. She ignores Jiri. "Give his lines to someone else," she says to me, shrugging herself into her knapsack. *His lines.* Like Jiri isn't there. "He won't learn them in time. The show's tomorrow. I don't want my TV debut wrecked."

Jiri shuffles his feet. Patti notices him now. "Look, Jiri, I'm sorry. But it's not working, you know. It's better for the show if you don't have anything to say. Don't you think so, Jane?"

Patti. Miss Gonsalves. Jiri. They all stare at me, waiting for my decision.

I wonder what I should do. What's best for Jiri? For the play?

The eyes decide me. Not Patti's or Miss Gonsalves' eyes, but Jiri's – they're hot, focused, deeply involved. I can't look away from them. I can't let them down.

"Jiri stays in," I say.

"Oh, no!" Patti appeals to Miss Gonsalves. "You're the boss. Can't you –"

"Are you sure, Jane?" Miss Gonsalves is surprised at the decision. Was it the wrong one? I want to do what's right, and I respect her so much.

"I'm sure," I say. She nods gravely.

Patti makes a little hiss of disgust and flounces away.

Jiri's face clears. "Thank you, Jane. Thank you. I will know them . . . soon."

"Tomorrow," I say. We're running out of soon.

"Tomorrow." He nods. "You are nice, Jane."

He reaches into his shirt pocket and pulls out a snapshot. "Are you sure you wouldn't like one of them?" The picture shows three kittens in a basket. Two black-and-white, one tabby. A ham-sized hand is stopping the tabby from climbing out of the basket.

"Very cute," I say.

An awkward moment at the dinner table. Big chocolate chip cookies for dessert – Grandma must have visited the bakeshop up the street. One cookie for Bernie, one for Bill, one for me, one for Grandma. We all thank her and dig in. She doesn't touch her cookie. It sits there on a plate in the middle of the table, a small piece of paradise. Is she going to wrap it up? Is she going to eat it herself? Bill and Bernie, finished already, eye the cookie. I'm chewing slowly, savoring, but I'm interested too – these are really good. Maybe we could have second helpings of paradise.

The radio is tuned to Grandma's station. Someone is explaining why the lady is a tramp. The cookie sits in solitary splendor. Mentally, I'm dividing it into three pieces. The boys lick their lips, leaning forward, like . . . I was going to say, like baby birds waiting to be fed, but I think they look more like pigs. Bernie especially, with his chocolate chin.

"You finished, William? Bernard?"

The boys look at each other, swallow, nod doubtfully.

"Then put away your plates." She helps Bernie out of his booster seat, hands him his plate. He walks to the counter. He looks back over his shoulder, then leaves. Bill has already gone. Now it's just me and Grandma, and the guy on the radio who loves Paris in the summer, when it sizzles.

Grandma hums along. I finish my cookie, every crumb.

"Thanks again," I say. "That was wonderful."

"You want the last cookie?" she asks.

I stare at it. Paradise all to myself. So why do I feel funny about accepting?

"I don't know," I say.

It's not that I mind having stuff all to myself. I don't need to share everything. But I haven't . . . well . . . *earned* the cookie. That's the word. If Bill and Bernie and I had flipped coins or counted fingers or played rock-paper-scissors, and I'd won, I'd be eating the cookie now. I might even be gloating as I ate it. But without any of these little rituals – part of my family life as far back as I can remember – then I don't deserve the cookie. It wouldn't be fair.

"I guess I'm not hungry," I say.

"Well, I wanted to let you know that I appreciate what you said this morning."

"When?" I don't know what she means.

"Say, do you like this song? This singer?"

I can see that she likes him. "He's okay," I say.

She takes a cardboard packet out of her pocket, opens it, and puts a mint in her mouth. A striped mint. Then she holds the packet out to me. "Humbug?"

"Um . . . sure." I'm not used to Grandma being nice to me. I take the humbug.

"Good."

For some reason I can take the humbug but not the cookie. Maybe because there are enough humbugs to go around.

Grandma starts rinsing the dishes. I suck away on my mint in silence for a moment, and then grab my knapsack and go up to my room.

On my bed is a record – not a CD, an old vinyl album. I know what they are, even though I don't have any. There's a picture on the front – a drawing – of a guy in a gangster kind of hat, holding hands with a lady in a long dress. *Sinatra Sings* is the title of the album. Whoever that is.

I don't understand. It must be Grandma's record, but what's it doing in my room? Why does she want me to have it? I turn it over. There's a song on the back called "I Love Paris."

I read the liner notes. I find out that Sinatra is the singer and his first name is Frank and he was pretty famous a long time ago.

How long ago? I hunt around and spot the date at the bottom right. 1957.

My artifact.

A noise from behind me. I look up. Grandma's in the doorway.

"Is this what you went back to your apartment for?" I ask.

She shrugs. "I'd play it for you, only there's no record player here."

We stare at each other for a moment. "Thanks," I manage at last.

"Don't scratch it," she says, and turns to go.

21

What If the Goat Has Kittens?

We live close to the school. Because the clocks in our house are fast – or else the ones in school are slow – I can leave at 8:50 by our kitchen clock, run down Garden Avenue, up Copernicus, and along Fern Avenue, and get to school before the 8:50 bell. That's what I usually do. But not today. Today is show day. I leave our house – and get to school – at 8:15. I want to check the scenery.

I find Mr. March in the main floor hall, and ask him to take me to the Electrical Room. Mr. March is one of my favorite people in the school. He's old and quiet. He has no hair on his head, but a whole lot on his arms. His eyes are big and dark. When he smiles, which he does often, you can see flecks of gold.

He's not smiling now. "Wanted to talk to you, Jane," he says, leading me downstairs. "It's about," he lowers his voice, "Mr. Gebohm."

"Oh, yes?"

Our school is really old. Built in eighteen hundred and something. The basement looks its age. Layers and layers of paint over brick and concrete. And it's a maze. Narrow corridors, blind turnings, dim lighting.

"What about Mr. Gebohm?" I say.

Mr. March selects the right key from a crowded ring on his belt. No fumbling for him. He holds the door of the Electrical Room open for me. It's a dusty space, with gray paint flaking off the walls and bare bulbs swinging overhead. One wall is lined with dials and those big hinged switches that Dr. Frankenstein pulls up to turn on the power in his laboratory. The air hums.

Old furniture and supplies are piled at the back of the room. That's where we're storing the *Nutcracker* scenery and costumes.

"What about Mr. Gebohm?" I ask.

"I don't really know how to say this," he says, "but I overheard him talking in the staff room. Have you been bothering Mr. Gebohm, Jane?"

"I guess so," I say. "I broke up his basketball practice the other night."

"Well, you shouldn't have. He's a vengeful man. He was talking about you yesterday. About how he was going to wreck your performance."

I knew it. I knew it. I stare up at Mr. March. "Mr. *Gebohm* said that?"

"SHHH, girl."

"He did?" I lower my voice. "How? How is he going to wreck my performance?"

"He didn't say."

"Well, who was he talking to?"

"Maybe himself. I don't know. I was outside the staff room, cleaning up some black marks on the floor. When I went in, the room was empty." He frowns, distracted for a moment. "You know, if I ever catch the person making those marks, I'll. . . ."

"What am I supposed to do?"

Mr. March shrugs. "Mr. Gebohm is a strange one. Caught him in here last night, you know. Don't know where he got a key. He was talking to himself then."

"Oh, no. The scenery. Maybe that's it!"

I picture the backdrops ripped to shreds, or defaced with graffiti. I drag them into the middle of the room and lay them out on the floor, side by side. The first one is the inside of the Stahlbaum house, with a window and a fireplace. At the big scene change, Michael pulls a string and the top sheet drops open to reveal licorice trees and pink bubblegum clouds and things like that. This is Candyland, where Maria and her Nutcracker Prince will reign happily ever after, if only Jiri can remember his lines.

I examine the backdrops carefully. They both look all right. I breathe a sigh of relief.

"Very nice," Mr. March comments. "But your twine is all knotted."

"Yes, that happened last night. Michael kept tugging and tugging."

"You want a quick release knot," he says. "Then the second whatsis here will fall with one pull."

He gets down on his knees to peer at the string. "Dear, dear. You got yourself quite a tangle here. Can you undo it?"

The phone rings, startling me. It's beside the door; I didn't notice it when I came into the room. It sounds as loud as the recess bell.

Mr. March gets slowly to his feet. I can hear his knee joints creak when he stands. Dad's knees do that too. "Hello," he says into the phone.

I pick up the twine. The knot is as big as my knuckle. It'll take me an hour to undo. And I don't have an hour. I do, however, have a pair of scissors. I reach into my knapsack.

"I'm with Jane Peeler, now, Mr. Gordon," says Mr. March. "Yes, about *The Nutcracker*. We're fixing some of the scenery. . . . Yes, sir, we want to look our best for the TV cameras. I'll be up there as soon as I finish down here."

He hangs up with a smile on his face. "Mr. Gebohm may want to wreck the performance tonight, but Mr. Gordon sure doesn't." Mr. March regards the broken twine with regret. "Well, that is one way to untie a knot. Let's get you some more twine."

The sign on the room next door says COAL CELL. I picture hunks of black rock, and bars. Mr. March opens the door. I'm wrong. The room is bright yellow and very clean. There's a sink and a long counter, a table, and two wooden chairs. On the table sit a radio and a book. On the counter sit a teapot and two cups. And a menorah.

"Sit down, Jane." Mr. March hunts through a drawer, finds tea bags, sugar, and twine. He plugs in the kettle, puts tea bags into a pot, and then cuts a length of twine.

I figure the chair with arms is Mr. March's. I sit on the other one.

The menorah has one candle in it. I remember what Grandma said yesterday.

"*Gut yontiff,*" I say.

Mr. March smiles. "Thank you. A happy holiday to you too." He cuts a length of twine and ties it in a big loopy knot. It doesn't take him long, but it looks complicated. The kettle is boiling. He hands the knotted twine to me, unplugs the kettle and pours.

"Would you drink tea with me, Jane? As a celebration of the holiday season. Eight days the lamps burned, when there was no oil. A great miracle."

I check my watch. 8:35. Plenty of time. "Thank you. I don't have tea very often."

Mr. March pours tea into both cups, adds sugar to one and pushes it across the table to me. I pull the loose end of the twine and . . . the knot comes apart in my hand. Instantly and completely, like a dropped egg. "Wa-hoo!" I say. "Talk about a miracle!"

He shakes his head. "Just a useful trick. Let me show you."

He takes the twine and loops it in his hand. I try to follow. He does it again. And again. And again. I sip the tea. He gives me the twine. I try to loop it the way he does. I can't do it. He shows me again. And again. Then it's my turn again. I do one loop, and then it falls apart.

He shows me again. I try. Nope. And I try again. And . . . this time I get it. The knot disappears in my hand. Wa-hoo.

"That's it," says Mr. March.

I do it again – pulling the knot apart, retying it, pulling on the loose end, and watching the knot fall to pieces. "Thanks, Mr. March," I say. "Thanks very much."

"No bother. Now, drink your tea and practice some more."

I tie the knot again. And again. And as I fiddle with the twine, I start to tell Mr. March about my troubles in school. And at home. Everything.

He listens attentively. When I tell him about Dad, he clucks his teeth sympathetically. When I tell him about the basketball practice, he shakes his head in admiration. "So that's what Mr. Gebohm was upset about. You are a formidable foe, Jane Peeler. But I would watch out for him all the same."

When I tell Mr. March about my problem with Jiri, he nods vigorously. "Good for you," he says.

"Did I do the right thing?"

"Oh, yes. You gave the boy a chance. That's good."

His certainty is comforting. I've been in such doubt. The tea is hot and sweet. It's comforting too. I put down my cup.

"But what if he forgets his lines tonight?" I ask.

"What if he remembers them? What if someone else forgets? My Aunt Sadie had a funny saying for situations like that. 'What if the goat has kittens?' she used to say, meaning that you can't foresee everything. You can only do your best."

We go back to the Electrical Room. He ties the two backdrops together with the new length of twine. I practice the trick knot one more time. It works perfectly.

"But, Mr. March, how can a goat have kittens?"

"It's just an expression. And, to be honest, Aunt Sadie was a strange old lady."

Two absentees in our class today. Michael will probably show up after lunch, yawning. He's done that before. But Jiri is away too – and he hasn't been late or absent all term.

Miss Gonsalves takes me aside during silent reading period. "It's about Jiri," she says in a low voice. She's wearing a black pantsuit. She looks like a panther with jewelry. "I hope you did the right thing, leaving him in the play. What if he forgets his lines tonight?"

"Well, what if Justin gets sick? Or you? What if Patti forgets all her lines?"

Miss Gonsalves frowns. She doesn't get it about the goat having kittens. "If Jiri's sick, that might solve our problem. You can give his lines to someone else."

22

Einstein Diet

I'm onstage, in the last period of the day, checking lights. There are separate rheostats for the reds, blues, greens, and yellows. These are the four kinds of colored lights on the grid.

Four hours until show time. No point in another rehearsal after school: either we have it now or we don't.

The gym door opens. I hear hall noise for a second, then silence as the door closes. I check my notes: *Scene 1: Red and yellow up, blue down.*

I turn out the houselights. The stage looks unnatural from up here. I wonder how it looks from out there. I jump down to the gym floor and practically bump into Zillah. She's in black – black shirt, black pants, black hair, black lips and nails. If she was dark skinned and frowning she'd be almost invisible, but her face is pale and her teeth gleam in a rare smile.

I smile back. "Oh, hi, Zillah."

She doesn't reply. Her head is on one side, like a bird's. She stares up at the stage. "Spooky," she says approvingly.

"Really?" It isn't supposed to be. It's the Stahlbaum house. Spooky is for later. "Stay there. Don't move." I run back to the stage, and dim the blues some more. "How does it look now?" I call.

"Spooky."

Maybe she's the wrong person to ask. To Zillah everything is going to be a shade of spooky. I make a note.

There is a light in Mr. Gebohm's office across the gym. I'm worried about him, but I have a job to do.

Zillah is clumping around in her heavy black shoes. Does she want to be friends with me? Is that why she came to the gym? I'm not used to this. Patti is my friend – was my friend. But that's because I've known her forever. Normally – last week, say – she and I would be checking the lighting cues. Zillah is a new friend. I don't know what new friends do.

"Do you want to help?" I ask.

She nods, shaking her hair out of her eyes.

"Then tell me how these lights look." I turn the houselights back off. Then I push up the blues for the midnight scene. "What's the effect now?" I ask.

"Spooky."

"How spooky?"

"Really spooky!"

"Good." I make another note.

Now there's only the scene in Candyland. *Houselights very low, red and yellow up, green medium.* I turn the dials. "How spooky is this?" I ask.

"Not very."

"Good."

When I turn up the gym lights, Zillah has moved closer to the stage. She's frowning, the way she usually does. You know, she should smile more. Her face is prettier when she smiles. She cocks her head, listening. I listen too. There is something coming from . . . underneath me.

Under the stage.

I shudder. I think about the mice in our house. I don't like the idea of animals living in my walls. In my floor.

Zillah opens the cupboard doors that lead under the stage. The school stores hundreds of stacking chairs there on big rolling dollies. Zillah opens the cupboard doors. "Aha!" she says.

Out crawl Michael and Jiri. They're covered in dust. So are their coats and knapsacks. Jiri smiles nervously.

"There you are!" I say. "You've been gone all day. What have you –"

Michael holds up his hand to stop me. He nods to Jiri, who clears his throat and declaims, in a loud voice:

"Welcome, Prince and Princess both,
From your travels East and Noth.

In Candyland the prospects please –
Sunshine, warmth, a gentle breeze,
And we use tissues when we sneeze."

The last lines of the play. Pronounced perfectly.
He's got them.

"Congratulations, Jiri!" I shake his hand.

"We've been practicing all day, in there," Jiri says.
"With a flashlight." He opens his knapsack to show me.

"That's great. You too, Michael."

Jiri smiles hugely, like a kid on his first two-wheeler.
Michael cracks his knuckles.

"You There! What Do You Think You're Doing?"

Mr. Gebohm, of course. He stands in the doorway
to his office. His face is ugly – well, it always is, of
course, but what I mean is that it's uglier than usual:
all red, and his lips are stretched thin so that you can
see his teeth between them. Not that he's smiling.

"Nothing," says Michael. An instinctive answer
when a teacher asks what you're doing.

"No, nothing," echoes Jiri.

But I see no reason to lie. "We're working on
tonight's show," I say. "Zillah and I are doing a light
check, and Michael and Jiri are practicing their
lines."

"Oh, it's you, *Peeler*." He really doesn't like me, and –
this is going to sound funny, because I don't like him
either – it hurts. "The show tonight. *The Nutcracker*.
Well, I hope you all enjoy it. Ha-ha-ha."

He starts to close the door, then notices what Zillah is wearing. "Don't You Know You're Not Allowed Here In Those Shoes?" he shouts. "Get Out!"

Does he mean get out of the gym, or get out of the shoes? I don't know. Neither does Zillah. She rolls her eyes. Mr. Gebohm stands there, vibrating like a tuning fork. An angry tuning fork. His face is redder than ever.

"Get Out! All Of You! Out Out Out!" Mr. Gebohm points dramatically at the door. I guess he means out of the gym.

I gather up my notes. Michael and Jiri and I move quietly in our indoor running shoes. Zillah clumps after us.

Dinner is take-out chicken. What a waste! I have no appetite. I'm too worried. The whole school will be there, kids and moms and dads, aldermen and trustees, and TV cameras. What if we stink? What if we don't stink, and they hate it anyway? What if Mr. Gebohm does something? I don't know what he'd do, but what if he does?

I take a teeny bite of a chicken wing and put it down. The first meal in days that Grandma hasn't cooked – which means the first meal in days that tastes halfway good – and I can't eat it.

"What's wrong, Jane?" Dad is eating with us. Another first – in a while. He's sitting at the head of the table. Grandma is beside Bernie, cutting up his chicken for him.

"Nothing. Just nervous, I guess."

"She's on a diet," Bill teases. Just because I mentioned that my jeans were getting tight.

"Am not." I hate diets. Imagine not eating chocolate cake because someone else thinks it's bad for you. The way I figure it, life doesn't give you too many chances at chocolate cake, and you should try to grab them all. Turning down lettuce doesn't matter. You know you'll see it again soon enough. And if your jeans get tight, buy another pair. Or wear a skirt.

"Your mother used to go on diets," says Grandma. I stare. I can't imagine Mom on a diet. She's so elegant. And she never seems to work at it. "Oh, sure. She ate nothing but grapefruit for a week, I recall."

"Yuck." Bill grabs another piece of chicken. He's eating fast, even for him. He seems nervous. How can he eat when he's nervous?

"Whoa, boy. Slow down," says Dad. "Your jaws are moving faster than light. They're just a blur."

"It's the Einstein diet," Grandma cackles. "If you eat fast enough, you finish dinner before you start it."

Dad's mouth opens in surprise. He laughs so hard he chokes. "Einstein," he sputters.

Grandma looks proud of herself.

Bernie drops his new toy. I haven't seen it before: a square wooden pyramid with a stick coming out of one end. There are funny marks on the sides. Grandma picks it up.

"Where'd you get that, Bernard?" she asks.

"Bill's friend gave it to me," says Bernie.

"A dreidel." There's a smile hovering on the edge of Grandma's face, like early morning light, before the sun bursts over the horizon. "I haven't seen one of these in years."

Bill stares at her. "Dreidel, that's right. How did you know?"

"I remember playing the game. You spin it, and pick up your prizes depending on which letter shows up." She turns it slowly in her hands "A great miracle happened here, right?"

"Prizes?"

"Well, we used to play for –"

The front door opens with a bang. Mom sweeps down the hall and into the kitchen, where we're all eating.

"You're up!" she says to Dad, and gives him a big kiss. "Oh, isn't that good!"

Dad smiles up at her face.

"And there's chicken for dinner!" calls Bernie. "That's good, too."

"Yes, it is." Mom pulls up a chair. "Oh, look, here's a . . . what are those things called again?"

"Dreidel," says everyone.

"Right." Mom stares around the table.

Dinner is over, and Bill is wearing his costume in the living room. His class is singing the "Twelve Days of Christmas" in the first half of the winter concert. Bill is wearing a T-shirt and a pair of gym shorts. A paper crown sits crookedly on his head.

"What are you supposed to be?" asks Dad. He's dressed too – going outside for the first time in days. The doctor said it was okay, as long as he took it easy.

"A lord-a-leaping," I say.

"Jane! It's a surprise!" Bill, furious, leaps at me. Not a very lordly leap. He kicks me in the knee.

Grandma and Bernie are sitting on the floor, heads bent low. "Your turn," says Bernie. Grandma twirls the dreidel.

"*Gimmel!*" she says.

"That means pick up everything, right?"

"Right."

"I didn't know you were Jewish, Grandma," says Bernie.

She snorts, without looking up from the game. There's a pile of candies in the middle of the floor. She pops one in her mouth. "I'm not. But I . . . well, before I met your grandfather, there was this nice Jewish boy who came to call."

"Mother?" Mom stands in the doorway. "What did you say?" A look of total surprise on her face.

"Oh, nothing."

Dad chuckles.

23

The Goat Has Kittens

I love the atmosphere of a school in the evening. The hallways are full, the desks are empty, the kids are running around with big grins on their faces. It's all so familiar, and yet different – because we're not at work. I wonder if offices are like this in the evening? I doubt it. When Mom gets home late, she looks like she's been working hard.

I feel like Mom right now. I have a list in my hand, and a million details to check. Does Michael have his eyepatch? Can Essa see out of her costume if she wears her hat to make her head bigger? Do *all* the toys have swords? Do *all* the mice have mouse ears? Yes. Yes. Yes. Yes.

Am I having fun? Not really.

What makes it worse, of course, is all the people who *are* having fun. The classroom is really noisy. Kids are standing on desks, pretend fighting, giggling, telling jokes, sharing snacks. I'd love to be part of it. I'd love to sit down with Patti and just giggle at all the pandemonium, and wait for a teacher to tell us what to do.

No, not Patti. She's not having any fun either. Her hair is way up in a princessy style – her mom must have helped. Patti keeps patting it, as if to make sure that, like the American flag, it's still there.

From the gym down the hall comes the faint echo of laughter, and applause. The show must be about half over. Bill will be in the audience now. You're allowed to sit with your parents when your class is done. It doesn't seem fair. Bill will see my show, but I won't see his.

We're on in a few minutes.

Oh-oh. There's the Mouse King's mask head, flying through the air. "Watch out!" calls Michael. He's the one who just threw it. The big mask falls to the ground. Michael laughs.

"Hey, watch out, there!" I sound like a teacher. I hate that.

"That's what I said," says Michael. I give him a look.

Miss Gonsalves comes in with a young-old man. His hair and clothes are young, but his face is old. He carries a portable video camera. Not the kind your mom and dad have – a real big one. Miss Gonsalves introduces him as Lance. He's the videographer with CITY TV.

Lance smiles and waves. His teeth are white and perfect, but his hand is wrinkled. He looks sharply around the classroom, and nods to himself. "Mice and nutcrackers," he says, in a gravelly voice. "'Kay, I got it."

Miss Gonsalves is holding some papers in her hand. "These are your permission forms," she calls out. "Has everyone given them back to me? Without a permission form, Lance can't use you."

He lifts the big video cam onto his shoulder. Then he takes it down and fiddles with a few buttons and dials. Then he hoists it back up to his shoulder again. He can support the whole thing with one hand.

"I'll wander around, get some school atmosphere. See you guys on the stage, 'kay?" he says. He makes a gun with his free hand, and shoots us. Then he leaves.

"'Kay," calls Michael.

Miss Gonsalves follows Lance out the door.

Brad is at my elbow. On his face is a look of utter terror. "That guy is from . . . CITY TV? He's going to *film* us?"

"Yes, didn't you know? Don't you remember Miss Gonsalves telling us about her friend at the station downtown?"

He starts to shake. "I can't go on," he whispers.

You'll never guess who pokes his head in the door next. No, not Dad. He's in the audience with Mom. Not Bernie. He's at home with Grandma.

It's Mr. Gebohm. His eyes are big and wild, and his jaw twitches. He steps into the room, and closes the door. We all quieten down. There's so much craziness coming out of him, it's like a force field.

"Watch this," he says, very softly, yet with a tremor in his voice like a volcano about to erupt. He reaches out his hand and, very deliberately, turns off the lights, so that the room is in darkness. Then he goes off into peals of laughter. "Ha-ha-ha-ha-ha-ha." Like a bad horror movie, only it's not funny. Not at all.

Mr. Gebohm keeps laughing. He can't stop laughing. On and on he goes, doubling over. I don't know what to do. No one says a word. Not even Michael. I think we're all a little bit scared, except for those of us who are really scared. Who knows how long the scene would have lasted, but the door opens behind Mr. Gebohm.

"Miss Gonsalves?" It's Mr. March. He flips the light switch. "Oh, sorry, Mr. Gebohm. I didn't know what was going on in here. I didn't see you in the dark," he says.

Mr. Gebohm stops laughing, straightens up. "Yes. In the dark." He draws his head up and marches out the door. He doesn't just leave, he exits.

Mr. March stares after him.

"What do you mean, you can't go on?" I whisper. Here I am worrying about Jiri and Mr. Gebohm, and it turns out Brad is the problem. The goat has had kittens.

"I can't. Not if we're going to be on TV. I didn't know we were going to be on TV. Why didn't someone tell me we were going to be on TV?"

"Miss Gonsalves told us at rehearsal – oh, wait. Were you late, that time? And, anyway, Patti's been talking about it for days."

"I don't always listen to everything Patti says, you know what I mean?" He tries to smile at me. Not much of a smile. He's too worried. "My mom watches the CITY TV news every night," he says.

"So what?"

"Don't you see, she can't see me onstage. She can't!!!"

Patti comes over then. "Hi, Braddie," she says, slipping her arm under his. "Do you want to go over our lines together at the end?"

He shakes off her hand, and starts taking off his Nutcracker uniform.

"Wait. Wait!" I say. "What is going on?"

His eyes are wild and scared. I grab him by the arm and lead him into a corner. "Brad, stop. Calm down. Tell me what is happening."

He's trembling. "It's . . . my mom," he says.

Isn't it always. Unless it's your dad. I have a clue, of course. "Is this anything to do with . . . filberts and almonds and pecans?"

He nods, swallows, and then it all comes out. He's been lying to his mom, telling her he was staying late to work on a science project with me instead of rehearsing. When she finds out he's been lying to her, especially when she finds out he's been *acting*, well, as Grandma would put it, there'll be shell to pay.

"Why?" I ask. "What's wrong with acting?"

He's a bit calmer now. Across the room Patti is glaring at me. She doesn't like the way Brad is leaning against me.

"It's my dad," he says.

Isn't it always. When it isn't your mom.

"What about him? I thought your parents were divorced. I've never seen your dad around. He doesn't live anywhere near here, does he?"

"No. He lives in Hollywood."

"Oh."

"He's an actor. He left Mom when I was little. Ran away to Los Angeles and changed his name. Mom has hated actors ever since."

"Oh."

"She keeps telling me how horrible actors are. How they're untrustworthy and fickle and heartless. I'm all she has left, she says. She's so afraid of losing me, she keeps after me to tell her all about myself. She can't stand not to know what I'm doing. She wants to know all about me. And I . . . I just want her to leave me alone." He covers his face with his hand. I think back to his mother's phone call.

Something hits me on the arm, and falls to the floor. I whirl around. The mouse king mask is lying next to us.

Quiet in the classroom.

Miss Gonsalves' calm voice comes through very clearly. "Oh, dear," she says.

She stands under the clock, with her hands on her hips. Next to her is Lance, the video guy. Michael is snickering. Patti is looking upset. I pick up the mask.

"Get your costumes ready, everyone, and line up by the door," says Miss Gonsalves. "We're onstage in five minutes."

Brad grabs my arm, hard enough to hurt. "So don't you see, I *can't* go out there tonight," he whispers. "My mom thinks I'm at a birthday party. I made up an invitation and everything. If she sees me on the news, she'll. . . ."

"Yes."

I try to think. Come on, brain! If only you could order ideas easily, like on the internet: point and click. *Add this brilliant brain wave to your shopping basket?*

Got one! "Okay. Come here." I grab his arm. The video guy is filming the class as they line up. He turns the camera on us. I put up my hand the way the lawyer does on the news, when the client is guilty. *No comment*, the lawyer says. "Wait a minute, Lance," I say.

"Huh?" He comes out from behind the camera. "What?"

"Brad here does not want to be in the news clip," I say. "When you're filming the show, you've got to keep him out of it."

"What part does he play?"

"He's the Nutcracker."

193

Lance frowns. "But that's the lead, right? I mean, the show is called *Nutcracker*, isn't it? I don't know that I can keep him out."

Brad groans. "You've got to, Lance," I say. "You see, Brad's mom hasn't signed his permission form."

"What?"

"Hey, that's right," says Brad.

"But I thought that everyone agreed," he says. He stares over at Miss Gonsalves, who is straightening mouse ears. "You said everyone had signed," he says.

"Not Brad," I say.

Up close I can see that Lance needs a shave. The hair on his head is dark, but his beard is gray. He sighs and nods to Brad. "I'll shoot around you. If you get in the shot by accident, I still have two hours to edit you out. 'Kay?"

"'Kay," I tell him.

"Let's go," calls Miss Gonsalves. Lance gets behind the camera again. Brad puts on his Nutcracker hat.

"Thanks, Jane," he says.

I have to ask him one question. "Is your dad famous?"

Brad shakes his head. "He does commercials sometimes. There was one for soap. He sent me a videotape of it last year. Mom found it in my drawer and threw it out."

24

One . . . Two . . . Three . . . Nutcracker!

Out at the front of the stage, the grade 6 recorder club is playing "Jingle Bells" – I think. Backstage, behind the curtain, we are getting ready. Rustles, whispers, giggles. I'm halfway up the stepladder, hanging the hinged backdrop, when the stage phone rings.

"Get that, someone!" I whisper. Essa is nearest.

The backdrop is going to be fine. I show Michael how to work the trick knot.

Essa listens, then hangs up. Her mouth is open wide. So are her eyes. She looks terrified. She runs over to me.

"Jane, Jane, it was . . . him."

"Who?" I ask. But I know.

"Mr. Gebohm!" she whispers. "He says he's going to stop our show in five minutes."

The cast crowd around us. On the other side of the curtain, the recorder club finishes. The audience claps.

Essa shivers in her mouse-gray bodysuit. "He has the power, he says. With one flick of a switch he's going to turn all the lights out on you, the way you turned them out on him." She stares up at me. "He thought I was you, Jane. He hates you. He said . . . terrible things."

One flick of a switch. He must be downstairs in the Electrical Room. I can picture the big Frankenstein switches on the wall. I know where he is. But the knowledge is no good to me. I can't get there in five minutes. Even if I could, I couldn't deal with him, not by myself. Would Miss Gonsalves . . . no, she's out front, getting ready to sit down at the piano. Would Michael and Jiri . . . no, there's no time. No time.

"What'll we do?" asks Patti, for all of us. "What'll we do, Jane?"

"I'm scared," says Essa. "We can't do a show in the dark."

The applause is dying down out front. Principal Gordon Gordon is at the microphone, introducing "the grand finale, the high point of the evening's entertainment." He's nervous. He hesitates over Miss Gonsalves' name.

Brad nods his head. "Essa's right. Maybe we should give up and go home."

There's a murmur of assent from some of the cast.

"But . . ." stammers Patti. "But, Braddie, the TV camera is out there."

He looks away with a shudder. He'll take any excuse not to go on. "That makes it worse, Patti. You don't want to make a fool of yourself on TV."

Patti doesn't reply. I think she'd rather look foolish, on TV, than smart, not on TV.

"Let's tell Miss Gonsalves," suggests Jiri.

"Let's find Gebohm, and make him say g'bye! Ha-ha-ha!" says Michael. Always the joker.

"No," I say. "There's no time."

Brad is starting to undo his costume. Déjà vu. Didn't I just deal with this?

"Stop!" I say, loud as I dare. Onstage, Gordon is talking about how special it is that the local TV station is here to record this moment for the ten o'clock news. Everyone should make sure to watch, he says. "Stop, Brad. Come close, everyone! Listen to me!"

I try to think of something to say. Something inspiring, something that will work.

Add this brilliant brain wave to your shopping basket?

"We are going to go ahead with the show," I say. "We don't have time to find Gebohm. We don't have time to explain everything to Miss Gonsalves or Mr. Gordon. It's up to us."

"But –" Essa starts.

I hold up my hand. "Are we going to fold just because of a phone call? What if Gebohm is bluffing?"

I don't think he is. But it's a place to start. "We've worked hard on the show. We are going to put it on." My tone is firm. I sound sure of myself. Actually, I'm not sure of myself at all, but these are the words that come to me. I stare across the dimly lit backstage area at the phone. It's just not fair. It shouldn't be this hard. Gebohm shouldn't have it in for us. For me. But he does.

"So we wait a few minutes, and then if the lights are still working, we go on?"

"No, Brad," I say. "That'll delay the show. We go on when Gordon finishes talking. And we put on the show, as we rehearsed."

"How can we move around in the dark?" asks Essa. "We'll bump into each other, or fall off the stage."

Details, details.

"If it's dark, we'll get a light," I say. I sound sure of myself, but I don't – just now – know where I'm going to find a light. *Don't ask me the question, Essa,* I plead silently. *Don't ask where I'm going to find a light.*

"Where are you going to find a light?" she asks.

I smile at her. Important to show confidence. No words come to me.

Jiri coughs gently. "I brought my knapsack back-stage," he whispers. "There's a flashlight inside. I used this flashlight when I was hiding under the stage, practicing my lines."

Thank you. Thank you. Thank you. If I had any lingering doubts about my decision to let him stay in the show, this removes them. "That's great, Jiri," I say.

But Essa is shaking her head. "I don't like it. There's still Mr. Gebohm to consider. I don't want a teacher being mad at me."

"I'm with Essa," says Brad.

There are murmurs of doubt. The cast is shifting from foot to foot.

I've had enough. "Shut up, Brad. And you too, Essa. I am not going to give up here. This show will go on. I don't know how, exactly, but it will. I know it. Do you understand? *I know it.* Same way I knew about our rehearsal here, last week."

"But if Brad isn't. . . ." Patti lisps at me.

"If Brad isn't here, we do *The Nutcracker* without him. I don't care. If none of you want to go on, I'll do the show myself, holding the flashlight. Do you understand? Get your knapsack, Jiri." He trots away.

I don't know about them, but I'm convincing myself. The show is going to happen. It must. I didn't realize until now how important it is to me. It's mine, after all – I wrote and directed it, lied for it, bullied for it, lost a friend over it. It's mine.

"Now, who's with me?" I ask. "Who's ready to go onstage in about a minute?"

Silence. And then, an unexpected voice.

"I'm ready," says Justin. He smiles at me, trim and tidy. And calm. It occurs to me that he's never caused me a minute of worry. He knew his lines first. He taught the dance steps. He's never missed a rehearsal. He's never complained about anything.

He turns to the rest of the cast. "She's right, you know. The show comes first. If you're worried about looking silly, you'll never be an actor."

Hero? Professional? Nice guy? Hard to say. I've never thought too much about Justin before, but I'm awfully glad to have his support now.

"Thanks, Justin. Now, come *on*, you guys – hands in!"

I hold out my hand, palm down. Justin puts his hand on top. Slowly, as if she wants to but doesn't know if she should, Patti reaches out and puts her hand on top of Justin's. I smile at her. She smiles back. It's as close as we've been in days. Then Zillah shrugs and puts her hand in. Michael and Jiri are next. Then the rest of them – mice and toys and citizens of Candyland – crowd around with their hands. I'm feeling squished.

Only Brad is left outside the circle. He sighs. "All right," he says. "All right." He puts his hand on top of the pile.

I feel that I've pulled a truck up a hill. "Now, let's have a cheer. Everyone together: *Nutcracker!* Whisper it. Ready? One . . . two . . . three . . ."

"*Nutcracker!*" An enthusiastic whisper.

"Good. Get ready now," I say. "Michael, you're on first."

I run to my position, offstage left. Jiri's flashlight fits beside the light board.

Gordon Gordon is pointing out that the lyrics were written by one of the Sunnyside School students. Applause. I can feel myself turning red. "A girl named. . . ." Gordon pauses awkwardly. He's forgotten.

"Jane Peeler!" cries someone from the audience, and then, in a quieter but still audible voice, "You ham fool."

Grandma? Grandma? What is she doing here?

Laughter.

"*Ahem.* And now, ladies and gentlemen, boys and girls: *The Nutcracker!*" The principal trips on his way down the steps to the audience.

The curtain rises on the Stahlbaum house on Christmas Eve. Reds and greens and yellows shine warmly down. So, not so warmly, does a single spotlight near the back, with a CITY TV stencil on the side. Miss Gonsalves begins the overture. You know it: *dah, dah-dah-dah* dah *dah,* dah *dah dah.* Michael keeps time, nodding his head as he counts the beats – twelve beats before he is to begin speaking. I count with him, in my head. One, two –

The phone on the wall over my head rings.

Good thing the music is loud. I jump for the receiver.

"Jane Peeler, is that you?"

"Yes," I whisper.

"The five minutes are up. Get ready." He laughs crazily.

With half my mind, I'm still counting with Michael onstage. Nine, ten, eleven –

On the next beat, the lights go out. All of them. My reds and greens and yellows. The CITY spot. Everything.

I drop the phone and flip the switches on the board. Nothing. Nothing at all. I try the houselights. Nothing. All you can see are little red dots – showing that the video cameras in the parents' hands are turned on – and the red emergency EXIT signs over the gym doors. And in a moment everyone will be filing through them. And our *Nutcracker* will never be seen.

A power failure. Mr. Gebohm's revenge.

I reach for Jiri's flashlight.

25

Time Is Odd Stuff

Time moves slowly. Very slowly. A great sinuous shape is time, writhing toward me, spiraling in on itself, revealing hidden treasure in every slowly passing coil. I am able, in a fraction of a heartbeat, to note my own feelings of shock and horror. And determination. My eyes widen, the hairs on my neck and arms stand up, my breathing quickens. My heart thuds like a hammer in my chest. All this in an instant, an eye blink. And that's not all I can do. My mind races forward, leaving counted time a long way behind.

Strangely enough my first thought is for Brad, waiting in the dark. Poor Brad, lying to his mom night after night, worrying all the time. I can't imagine the Nutcracker Prince doing that. Maybe he wasn't such great casting, after all. Funny, I used to think he was kind of good-looking, with his golden hair and lazy smile. No longer.

I wonder if Dad is in the audience? He said he was coming. My poor dad. I have a vivid picture of

Grandma whacking him on the leg with the broom.

It's as dark as the inside of a toothpaste tube. I think of all the work that's gone into the show. Me reading the *Nutcracker* story back in September, and then writing a poem and showing it to Patti. And her eyes lighting up, and then her saying what a great idea it would be if I could write some more poems and turn them into a *Nutcracker* play, and she could star in it. And Miss Gonsalves saying she would help us put it together, and play the music. I think of the rehearsal saga this past week, culminating in the battle for the gym.

A flash of guilt. The whole fiasco is my fault. If I hadn't been so pushy at the basketball practice, would Mr. Gebohm have wanted this revenge?

A flash of fear. Essa's right: he really does hate me. That's awful.

A flash of itchiness. I want to scratch my nose. I can't think about that. I haven't time to think about that. But I am itchy.

These thoughts zoom by. The mind moves faster than a striking rattlesnake. Time doesn't. Time is a bigger snake altogether, a sleepy anaconda, coiling lazily around me. Has a second passed? A single second? No, not yet. Time is odd stuff.

I think of Bernie and Grandma sitting in the darkness. Nice of them to give up their dreidel game to come.

Miss Gonsalves knows the overture by heart – she doesn't need to see the notes. How long has she been playing in the dark? Has she reached the next note yet? There it is. I hear it, the twelfth beat of the overture to Tchaikovsky's *The Nutcracker*, as arranged for piano.

I picture myself running downstairs to confront Mr. Gebohm. I sneak out the door at the back of the stage and run like the wind and fall down the basement stairs. I crack my head open, and lie there in a pool of blood. No one finds me until Mr. Gebohm turns the lights back on. I suffer a horrible concussion, and have to go to hospital for weeks and weeks. Mr. Gebohm visits me, and steals my grapes.

I think about him down in the Electrical Room, gripping the power switch with his meaty hands, his eyes flashing behind his little glasses. And I find myself thinking of the man who works in the basement. Mr. March is calm, generous, good – all things that Mr. Gebohm is not.

Another note from the piano. The audience is quiet. Not a cough, not a whisper, not a scrape as a chair is pushed back.

I think about Bernie's dreidel game. What did Grandma say? *A great miracle happened here.* And I wish . . . well, it's no good wishing. I have to act. Jiri's flashlight is in my hands.

The atmosphere in the gym is hot and sweaty. The little red dots on top of the video cameras are still.

They make me think of lights on a Christmas tree. We always put our tree in the living room. Dad lifts one of us up to put the star at the top of the tree. Last year, Bernie jumped out of Dad's arms and knocked the tree over.

I think about Grandma, lending me her Frank Sinatra record. I think she likes me. As much as she can like anyone.

Zillah's artifact from the 1950s is going to be a hair dryer that you sit under. It comes in a suitcase and it's made of plastic and it takes half an hour to dry your hair. Half an hour! We had a good laugh over that at recess today. Actually, I had a good laugh. Zillah smiled.

Someone coughs. I hear it in slow motion, like a thunderclap rolling across the desert, reverberating around canyon walls before dying quietly away in the distance. It reminds me of the way my dad would cough, last week.

I think about the mice in our house. None in the mousetraps. I wonder if they're gone? I wonder what we should do about it? I want to get rid of them, but I don't want to use mousetraps, or poison.

And on the subject of poison, what am I going to do about Patti? We've had a lot of fun together; we've laughed and held hands and gone to each other's birthday parties and done all our shared projects together . . . and it turns out that she really doesn't like me. Maybe she never did. Funny, huh? I can feel the prickle of tears at the corners of my eyes.

I come to the conclusion – funny that, after thinking about Patti for days, I should reach the conclusion now, in this busy second of time – that she can't be a real friend. Real friends don't talk badly about each other. They don't lie to each other, or involve each other in their own lies. Which means, I guess, that Brad isn't a real friend either. Brazil nuts, indeed!

Time to act. I'm gripping Jiri's flashlight tightly. I point it at the stage.

And then, just like that, the lights come back on. My odyssey of thoughts – of Grandma and Dad, of Patti and Brad, of Christmas and Chanukah, of Miss Gonsalves and Mr. Gebohm, of mice and nutcrackers – has taken one second. About the length of time it would take to blow out a match.

I scratch my nose vigorously.

26

It Doesn't Matter

The lights are on, and time starts acting up again. It doesn't move slowly. Now it dashes forward like a jackrabbit. My mind, meanwhile, has turned into a tortoise, unable to catch up.

I scratch my nose some more. I stare at the lights. So bright. So surprising. Something is different – and wrong. What is it? Must think . . . .

"Hey, Jane!" whispers Patti. She's beside me, dancing with impatience. "The lights! Turn them off!"

"Huh?"

"What's wrong with you?"

Oops. The houselights are on. I flipped the switch when the power went down. Now all of the power is back, and the gym is bright. I slam down the houselights, and flick back to the reds and greens. Patti stomps into position.

In a very steady voice, Michael calls to the wings:

"Fritz and Maria, come and view
The genius of your god-papa.
No one else could bring for you
A Christmas gift so odd. Ha-ha!"

All right, so I'm not Shakespeare. But Michael does a good job delivering the lines so that they rhyme, and the audience laughs. They actually laugh.

What a feeling! *A roomful of people like what I wrote.*

It's going to work out. I know it. I know it. Suddenly I'm ten feet tall. I'm totally in control. Patti and Justin are out now. The audience is still laughing. The show goes on. I run around backstage on silent printless toe, herding the rest of the cast into position. I anticipate all the scene changes, flicking the lights in perfect time. I don't need my clipboard. I can see the whole play at once, from any angle, like one of those 3D computer models. I can manipulate it all with a flick of my hand. I can fly.

The audience keeps laughing. I can make out Grandma's amused cackle from backstage. Once heard, never forgotten.

The big transformation scene goes well – a full-sized nutcracker appearing as if by magic from under the table when I change white lights for reds. The audience applauds.

Brad does a good job marching about the stage, but I notice he swings his arms much higher than in rehearsal, hiding his face from the TV camera.

Patti, on the other hand, spends a lot of time at the front of the stage. She wants the TV camera to find her. When she comes off, I tell her to move more upstage.

"Why?" she pouts.

"When you talk from downstage, you turn your back to the audience. Don't you want them to see your face? Now, get ready. You're on in . . . four seconds."

She shuts her mouth, and does what she's told.

The phone is still off the hook. I can hear a confused gabble of noise from the receiver. I hold it to my ear.

It's Mr. Gebohm. He's . . . well, talking crazy talk.

"I guess they've all left now, eh, Peeler? Your show is ruined! My revenge complete. Ha-ha-ha-ha-ha." Hysterical laughter. I put down the phone.

The battle between the toys and the mice is raging. Brad swings mightily with his new sword in both hands – and one of the Mouse King's heads falls. It's hanging by a thread – right in front of Essa's eyeholes. The audience claps, covering Essa's scream for help.

She stands there in the middle of the mêlée. The scene should last a bit longer, but it won't now. Essa's afraid to move. Brad looks for me offstage. I catch his eye, and make the cut gesture, finger across my throat. Then I kill the lights for a second. The action stops, and when the lights come back up, the Mouse

King is lying on the stage with the Nutcracker's sword through the hole where the head was glued.

Brilliant improvisation. Brad has acting in his blood, all right.

The change of backdrop goes without a hitch, and the happy couple – Fritz and Maria – are now ready to reign in Candyland. Up the yellows, down the blues. The cast makes an aisle, and kneels. Brad and Patti, arm in arm, walk down the aisle toward a large figure in a striped robe and turban. The Herald of Candyland raises a hand in greeting.

Jiri is facing stage left, to me. I can see his eyes flicker once, twice, and I know – *I know* – that he has forgotten his lines. He clears his throat and begins: "Welcome, er, welcome royalty."

And stops. Yup. Wrong line. But you know what? It doesn't matter. So much has happened in the last few minutes that I'm past caring about little things, such as Jiri forgetting his lines. It's been a great show. I'm proud of myself, proud of us all. No matter what happens now, I've had a wonderful time. I give Jiri the thumbs-up. He closes his eyes, and in a clear bell-like voice, recites a verse I never wrote – a brilliant brand-new ending made up on the spot:

"Welcome, welcome, royalty
From every girl and boy-alty
Who lives in Candyland!
You will command our loyalty

Our jollity, our joy-alty,
Forever after you will see
That living here is *grand*!"

A giant smile splits Jiri's face across the middle. He bows deeply. The music ends with a triumphant *dah duh dah duh* dah. And the crowd erupts like a kicked beehive.

Minutes later they're all still buzzing. We've taken our bows. (Even me – they called me out for a special one.) Lance has packed up his lights and camera and gone back to the studio. We're starting to file off backstage. I find myself beside Justin. I congratulate him on a fine show, and thank him again for his support before.

He ducks his head. I used to think he was shy; now I realize he doesn't want to give much away. "I guess Mr. Gebohm was bluffing after all," he says. "He never did shut off the power, did he?"

"I don't know," I say.

The principal is thanking the parents for coming, wishing everyone a happy holiday season. Suddenly, dramatically, the doors to the gymnasium are thrown open.

"Excuse me! Excuse me, please! Mr. Gordon. Mr. GORDON!"

It's Mr. March. "I found the cause of the power outage, sir," he says.

Dead silence. Then, into the microphone – the working microphone – Gordon says, "What are you talking about? What power outage?"

"I think you'd better come to the basement, sir. Something has happened."

27

A Great Miracle Happened Here

The principal tells the audience to stay seated and stay calm, but he might as well have told the rain to stay in the sky. Mr. March leads a crowd of staff, students, and parents down the stairs.

"*There*, you see." The caretaker points to the basement floor. It's light gray and very clean, except for a set of definite black marks. They form a trail, leading down the basement corridor.

"I don't understand," says Mr. Gordon.

"Someone was down here, wearing horrible boots with marking soles. I saw the marks in the flashlight, and I knew."

"Flashlight?" says Gordon.

"The trail goes right to the Electrical Room. Now, I swept the floor myself this afternoon, and there were no marks then. So I knew that a stranger had been down here. And I figured that the stranger was responsible for the power failure. I thought it might be a student – I've seen these marks on the halls

214

upstairs. So I went right into the Electrical Room, and –"

"Wait. What power failure?"

Mr. March stares around. "The power failure tonight. Just now. The power failure we've had for the last half an hour. That's why I was carrying a flashlight."

Gordon Gordon looks upset. "What are you talking about? There's no power failure."

"Well, not now, sir. Of course not. I turned the power back on. But he had the main switches pulled down. The whole school was blacked out."

It's hard for Mr. March to believe that we don't know what he's talking about. But the faces crowding the basement hallway show the same surprise. We all agree. There was no power failure. Not in the gym, anyway. Mr. March shakes his head.

"Well, that is strange," he says finally. "I was in the dark down here. I followed the marks, and there he was. He had a flashlight too. Here, I'll show you."

He leads us down the twisting hallway. The door to the Electrical Room is open. I worm my way to the front. The place is a lot messier than it was this morning. Boxes have been thrown around, and there's litter all over the floor. We crowd around the open doorway. Mr. March goes in. He finds a flashlight among the mess, and holds it up. "There!" he says. "See?" He tries to turn it on. It doesn't work. "Must have got broken in the scuffle," he says.

"Scuffle?" says Gordon. "Who did you fight?"

"Whom," says a voice from the middle of the crowd. Teachers. Gordon blushes.

"Whom, then," he says. "And where is he now?"

I try to picture the fight. Total darkness, except for flashlights zapping their beams of light all around. Just like a *Star Wars* movie. Mr. March doesn't look much like Anakin Skywalker, but beneath the bald head and chubby body beats a heart every bit as pure. I notice that the telephone is off the hook.

"I put him next door," says Mr. March.

"What's that noise?" asks someone's dad – a really tall thin guy, with long arms like a spider. "Sounds a bit like . . . singing."

"Stand back." Mr. March pulls a big ring of keys from his belt, and opens the door marked COAL CELL.

A strange figure is standing on the table in the middle of the room. A ginger-haired figure, with broken glasses and a ripped T-shirt, and wild staring eyes. He holds his arms over his head, making a big letter *O*. He laughs when he sees us all, and continues singing a song. It's the teapot song, only it isn't – not the way he sings it:

"I'm a basketball; I'm short and round.
Here is the basket, here is the ground.
When I hit the backboard, I rebound,
No, No, Do The Drill Again!"

"Coach?" says a familiar kid – a tall kid standing next to the spider-guy. "Coach, is that you?" Of course, it's Gill, the captain of the basketball team.

"I'm a little jump shot, falling true,
Right through the hoop and score it two.
Clang! I miss, and the crowd goes *boo*.
No, No, Do The Drill Again!"

He sees me then, and turns to point right at me. I can feel his craziness like a suffocating blanket.

"Ha! You!" says Mr. Gebohm. "I Did It! I Stopped Your Show, Peeler! I Did It! No *Nutcracker* For You. Hahahahahahahaha!!"

I stare at him and try to feel triumph. I try to feel anger. I can't do it. All I feel is sorry. I swallow. I want to cry. I want to run away.

I stumble backwards into someone's arms.

"There, there, honey." She clasps me tight and spins me around so that she is between me and Mr. Gebohm.

"Mom!" I close my eyes against tears. "Where did you come from?"

Her suit is mussed from the crowd of people. Her hair is mussed too. She smells like a goodnight kiss from when I was little. "I was here all along," she says.

Mr. Gebohm pirouettes on the top of the table, and begins his teapot song again. Gill's dad pulls him away from the door. Gill protests. "But that's Coach Gebohm!"

"Stay back. You too, Flip," Gill's dad says to a small skinny boy behind him. The small boy doesn't move. "Flipper, I mean it!"

Flipper must be Gill's brother. Would you believe it? His parents did name them both after parts of a fish.

"Oh, dear," says Mr. Gordon. "What will we do?"

"Phone the police," says one voice.

"Phone the hospital," says another voice.

I get a last look at the room where Mr. March and I had tea this morning. The radio is on the floor. Our cups are on the counter. The menorah has two candles in it. Mr. March closes and locks the door. Mr. Gebohm is still singing.

Upstairs again and time to go home. The crowd is breaking up. I'm holding Mom's hand. Dad is yawning, almost asleep on his feet. Bernie is asleep in Grandma's arms.

A bulky man moves smartly toward me. His head is large and round, kind of like his stomach. He's dressed like a salesman, but he's not selling. His eyes are warm and brown, and his smile is sincere. The hand he holds out to me is the size of a shovel.

"You're Bill's sister, aren't you?"

I smile politely. "Bill's sister" is not the way I think of myself.

"I want to congratulate you on a great show. You should be proud of yourself." Before I can thank him he turns to my parents. "Your daughter is very talented," he says. Before she can thank him he calls over his shoulder. "Come on, David!"

Oh, *that's* who he is. I've never met David's dad before. Of course, Bill is with David.

Grandma has Bernie tucked into his stroller. She's frowning at a NO SMOKING sign on the wall.

Mr. Bergmann and Mom are chatting about the boys. "He has the makings of a real scholar," he says. "You should see him and my David studying the Bar Mitzvah text together."

"Oh, yes?" says Mom.

"Bedtime!" says Mr. Bergmann. "It's after 9:00 already."

"Aw, Daddy. It's just 8:30 – look." David points to a clock overhead. It says 8:30 all right. So does the clock by the front doors of the school.

"My watch says 9:00," says Mr. Bergmann.

"Maybe your watch is wrong Mr. B," says Bill.

"My watch says 9:00 too," says Mom.

Did Mr. Gebohm turn off the power, or not? If he did, how come the lights stayed on in the gym? I'm confused, but too tired to worry about it.

A police car and an ambulance are pulling up to the school as we leave. "Hey, look!" says Bill, nudging me in the ribs. I hate that. "David and I were running up and down the hall after the show. What happened? Did we miss something?"

"Mr. Gebohm went crazy, and turned off all the power. Mr. March locked him in the basement. Now the poor guy thinks he's a basketball."

"No, really, what happened?"

Dad goes to bed as soon as we get home. I'd like to go too, but I force myself to stay up another hour, so I can watch the CITY TV news with Mom and Grandma.

I'm afraid of anticlimax. I'm afraid it will be like watching a tape-delay of a game my team has already won. I'll cheer, but there'll be no thrill.

But it's not like that at all. When the news theme starts, I'm on the edge of my seat. When Lance introduces our segment, I'm so excited I can't breathe. There's the gym. And the stage. And I realize: that's *my* show on the screen. I was part of this. And now here's Jiri's huge smile as he tells me – and the rest of the viewing audience – that "living here is grand." Mom winks at me. Grandma sucks hard on a minty humbug.

You know, Jiri's right.

28

Loose Ends . . .

I don't have much more to say. I can't tie up all the loose ends in my life because it's going on right now. Our Christmas tree is up, and it looks great. This year I got to put the star on the top. Has Grandma gone home? Not yet, because Dad isn't quite better, and we still need someone to take care of us while Mom works late. The idea, I think, is that Grandma will stay with us until Christmas and then go back to her apartment. Miss Gonsalves really liked the Sinatra record. Her mom had the same one.

Has Grandma stopped smoking? Of course she has. And if you eat the crusts of your sandwiches, your hair will grow curly.

Brad has gone to visit his dad over the Christmas holidays. I don't know where. Did he ever tell his mother the truth about our nut project? I don't know that, either. She hasn't called me since.

Patti and I are still not best friends. I called her once to say hi. She asked how I was doing. Fine, I said.

I ran into Jiri and Michael at the mall. I told Jiri, again, how much I liked his ending to *The Nutcracker*. He said, again, how sorry he was that he didn't remember his lines. His mind went blank onstage, and then the words just . . . appeared. Like a gift on the doorstep, he said. I told him I knew what he meant, and waved good-bye. Jiri waved back. Michael made a gun with his hand, and shot me good-bye. I wonder if he thinks this is suave?

Bill and David *are* still best friends. They play sailors together at our house, and study at David's. Bill likes to show off his Hebrew words. David gave him a *kipah* to wear when they go to temple. Apparently *kipah* is the real name for the beanie. I didn't know that – I thought it was called something else. I bought Bill a naval telescope for Christmas. I wonder if maybe I should take it back and get him a menorah instead. Mind you, a menorah makes an odd Christmas present.

I don't know if we still have mice, but I suspect so. We've never caught any in the traps, but last night I had another bowling dream. I wonder if those kittens of Jiri's are still available. I'll ask him next term.

ALSO BY RICHARD SCRIMGER

The Nose from Jupiter
Mild-mannered and shy, Alan Dingwall is not big or
strong. He hates soccer, can barely survive math, and
is a moving target for every bully in school. But all
that changes when Norbert, an alien from Jupiter,
moves into Alan's nose.

A Nose for Adventure
Alan's first trip to New York City begins badly. His
father isn't at the airport to meet him, and then
Frieda – a girl he met on the plane – is almost kid-
napped. Before long, smugglers are chasing Alan and
Frieda through the streets of Manhattan. Fortunately
help is on the way when Norbert comes to the rescue!

The Way to Schenectady
Jane Peeler is embarking on a typical family car trip.
But during a stop at a gas station, Jane meets Marty,
a kind, penniless, old man with a problem: he needs
to get to Schenectady for his brother's memorial
service the next day. Jane's plan to help Marty reach
his destination leads the family on a hilarious detour.